Loki's Curse

By A J Miller

I0621180

ISBN - 978 0 9957926 1 6

Published by Deep Dark Forest 2018

www.deepdarkforest.net

Chapter 1 - Ice Rider

The rider halts at the gatehouse. The grey tower rises high into the winter sky, its stones grimy with soot and frosted with ice. In past times the heads of traitors were paraded on the battlements at the top, left there to rot as a warning to all who pass into the King's City. There is nothing on the battlements now but a single scruffy crow who glares down at the rider with glittering, night-dark eyes.

Two guards in heavy overcoats stand to one side of the gate, warming their hands at a brazier of smouldering logs. They take in the rider's travel stained cloak and a broad brimmed black hat, the mud splattered grey horse and the chestnut mare who comes behind on a rope. With a horse like that, the traveler must be wealthy. The guards wave the rider on through the city gates and return to their fire.

Ruby breathes a sigh of relief and urges Molly forward. If the guards had known the price on her head then things would have gone differently. Each gate and checkpoint brings fresh danger but her disguise has served her well so far. Even if she were not a fugitive from justice, the high roads of England are dangerous for a lone traveller. The only place more perilous is London itself, the city whose gate Ruby has just passed under.

On the far side of the gate rises the span of London Bridge. The sun is not yet risen and the way ahead is

3

dim. Tall houses have been built along both sides of the roadway and the ramshackle buildings loom over her like cliffs, leaning in at crazy angles, giving the way ahead the forbidding look of a tunnel. Painted wooden signs hang above the doorways; angels, eagles, elephants and magpies, falling stars and fierce eyed kings, glimmering in the half-light like fugitive fragments from a dream.

A lantern flares up, sending shadows dancing over the decaying house fronts, and a man appears at a doorway. He jams a wooden crutch into his armpit and comes hopping over the icy cobbles, scuttling nimbly round the piles of dirty snow, his lantern swinging in his hand. He comes to a halt in front of Ruby and she reins in her horse.

"Spare a penny for a crippled soldier? One who lost his leg in the service of King and Country."

The man is dressed in threadbare coat the colour of mud and his single shoe is held together with string. His cheeks are hollow with hunger and his lips are blue from cold. He looks up at the rider with an imploring expression.

"Please, sir. I've a family to feed."

Ruby will have to make the money in her purse last if her quest is to succeed. But what use is wealth if you do not share it? She reaches into her cloak and throws down a coin. It flashes in the lamplight like a falling star and vanishes into the beggar's outstretched hand. The man opens his fingers and gasps to see a golden guinea. Enough to feed his family for a month.

"Thank you, sir -" the old man stops when he sees Ruby's face; her hazel eyes and long brown hair. "God Bless you, My Lady," he mumbles, shuffling back to let her past.

Ruby pulls her hat brim down; it is better for people to think that she is a man.

The darkened windows of the ramshackle houses are not as empty as they might seem and rumours are already spreading in the shadows of the lone traveller with gold to spare. Long before Ruby has crossed the bridge the news of her coming has reached the ears of Mr. Famish, sitting like a spider at the heart of his whispering web in his attic room above the Raven Inn. The master thief narrows his eyes and issues instructions to the pale faced messenger boy who stands trembling before him.
"What are you waiting for?" Famish hisses, reaching out a bony hand towards Jimmy Twigg's face. The fingernails are long and yellow, their curved points as sharp as needles. "You have your orders. Get to it - before I rip your eyes out!"
Mr Famish smiles to himself as Jimmy Twig bolts down the stairs. He rises from his armchair and steps to the window. He pulls aside the ragged curtain and peers down at the road below.

There is a gap between the houses at the middle of the bridge and Ruby halts to look out over the river. The Thames is a solid mass of ice, dotted with the beetling shapes of tiny boats. The bigger ships lie helpless and icebound along the banks but the boatmen have fixed runners to the bottoms of the smaller craft and are punting them over the frozen river with poles, ferrying goods and passengers unwilling to make the narrow and dangerous crossing by the bridge.

Along the river's frozen bank sprawls London, smoking and groaning in the dawn like a great dragon waking from sleep. Ruby gazes in wonder at the endless stretch of snow covered rooftops and the countless church spires, rising dark into the winter sky. There are more houses here than she has ever seen before and more people than she can imagine. The only landmark that she can guess at is the dome of St. Paul's Cathedral, rising through the veil of mist to catch the first rays of the rising sun.

Ruby has come to find her family. After that, she must begin her impossible search. The hope that she might find help in London is all that has sustained her in the long days of riding but now that she sees the vastness of the city she feels only dread. She understands forests and moor tops, she has walked under the stars of Faerie and talked with the Queen of Twilight, but London is another thing entirely. Where in this great rat warren should she start looking?

Ruby turns away and urges her horse on. There is nothing to gained in gawping and wondering; her life depends upon the task ahead, and Davey's too.

Despite the bitter cold and the early hour, the crossroads on the far side of the bridge is crowded with market stalls, carts and carriages. People on foot grumble at Ruby as she edges her way forward. The crowd thickens, jostling and pushing. A hand takes hold of Molly's bridle and someone grabs Ruby's leg and pulls, trying to topple her from her horse. She kicks out and draws her pistol.

"I'll shoot the next one of you who gets in my way!" she shouts.

A woman screams and the press of people pull away. The grabbing hands are drawn swiftly back and Ruby sees two hooded men pushing away into the crowd. The road ahead clears and Ruby kicks Molly forward. At once, she senses something wrong; she turns to look back over her shoulder and sees the halter rope hanging limp from the back of her saddle; Dervish is gone! The attack on Ruby was just a distraction, the thieves were after the chestnut mare.

Ruby gazes wildly about. There are carriages and horses everywhere and it is hard to see clearly in the half-light of dawn. She hears a whinny of fear and turns just in time to catch a glimpse of Dervish disappearing down an alley. A man lies low on her back, spurring her forward with a whip and gripping onto her mane with his free hand. Ruby gives a cry of rage and kicks Molly into a gallop.

"Out of my way!" she yells, and the remnants of the crowd scatter.

Molly turns into the alley and Ruby has to duck to avoid cracking her skull on a hanging shop sign. She crouches low, her face pressed against Molly's neck, as they dodge their way along the alley. Up ahead, Dervish is already turning into another side street.

"Faster," Ruby hisses into Molly's ear.

The narrow streets twist and turn like a maze and Ruby knows that she will have to keep Dervish in sight if she is to have any hope of rescuing her.

Her heart clenches as she sees a cart full of barrels being pushed out into her path. The men at the back of the cart dive for cover but there is no time for her to stop.

"Jump for it!" calls Ruby.

Molly gives a great kick and leaps over the wagon. Her back hooves crash into the barrels, sending them bouncing away over the cobbles. Molly skids around a corner and Ruby catches sight of Dervish again. The chestnut mare is faster than the grey coach horse but in the narrow lanes the rider cannot make full use of her speed.

Three more breathless turns bring them onto a cobbled dockside. Out on the frozen river the sun glimmers gold on the ice. The thief gives a whoop of delight and whips Dervish hard, urging her into a terrified gallop. Ruby bites back her rage and concentrates on keeping as close as she can. The horse thief looks back over his shoulder and flashes Ruby a sneering grin.

"You'll not catch me now!" he laughs.

They race on, between tall warehouses and the looming shapes of icebound ships. Dervish pulls steadily away from Molly and Ruby is beginning to think that all is lost, until Dervish's rider brings her to a sudden, skidding halt. The way ahead is blocked by the open doors of a warehouse and a cart piled high with bales of cotton. On one side is the warehouse wall and on the other a cobbled slipway running down to the frozen river. The man wheels Dervish about, kicks her down the slipway and gallops out onto the ice.

Is he insane? They will both be drowned.

But the rider knows exactly what he is doing; the ice is several feet thick and quite strong enough to take a horse's weight. Dervish gallops on, the ice surface splintering up under her hooves as Ruby gazes after them in mute wonder.

Beneath the arch of the bridge the shadows of men and horses move in the mist. There are wagons and carts and, further out, a line of market stalls have been built directly onto the ice. Ruby remembers a tale that her father once told her, of the Frost Fair, held on the frozen Thames when the ice grows thick enough.

Ruby urges Molly down the slipway after Dervish. Molly is badly spooked by the ice but she does as Ruby asks, galloping for all she is worth, the thunder of her hooves echoing like drumbeats in the depths of the frozen river. The horse thief turns to glance back over his shoulder and Dervish skids and stumbles. She rights herself and the rider whips her on. Ruby sees the blood on Dervishes flanks and gives a snarl of rage. She would like to take out her pistol and shoot the thief but the risk of hitting Dervish is too great.

The crazy chase cannot last long. Molly's hooves are slipping beneath her and it is only a matter of time before one of the horses loses its footing. A fall onto the iron hard ice would be deadly.

Should she let Dervish go?

There comes a sudden splintering sound and a tremor shiverers through the ice. A crack opens ahead of Dervish, widening almost at once into a jagged chasm of dark water. Dervish shrieks in terror and skids to such a sudden halt that the thief is sent tumbling forward over her head. He lands hard on the ice and slides into the icy water with a splash.

Ruby brings Molly to a stop beside Dervish. She takes hold of the chestnut mare's bridle and puts her hand on her neck. Dervish is trembling with terror and blood is running from the whip cuts in her flanks.

"Easy now," whispers Ruby. "I won't let him hurt you any more."

Dervish calms under Ruby's touch. She snorts and tosses her head, telling Ruby exactly what she thinks of riding on the ice.

The ice has stopped cracking and the horses are still. The thief is trying to pull himself out of the water but his frozen hands can't find a grip and he keeps slipping back. Ruby stares down at him in a rage.

"You whipped my horse bloody," she snarls. "I've half a mind to let you drown."

"Please miss!" The thief gives a whimper of terror and falls back into the water. He sinks and comes up again, gasping and choking. His lips are blue with cold and he is thin and starved looking. He's no older than Ruby; fourteen at the most.

Ruby slips down from Molly's back, unhooks the spare lead rope from her saddle bag and loops one end around the pommel of Molly's saddle. She throws the other end to the drowning boy who grabs it in his trembling hands. Ruby leads Molly back, the rope goes taut and the thief is hauled out of the freezing river. He climbs to his feet and shakes himself like a dog, sending water sluicing out over the ice around him.

Ruby takes out her pistol and points it at the shivering boy.

"If I ever hear of you whipping a horse that way again, I will shoot you," she says.

The boy nods his head. His skin is as pale as the ice beneath his feet and his teeth are chattering uncontrollably.

"Run home to your mother," she says. "You'll freeze to death if you stand here a moment longer."

The boy doesn't need telling twice. He stumbles away into a sliding run, heading past Ruby and back toward the dock.

Ruby leads Molly and Dervish back to shore on foot. The rising sun is dazzlingly bright and their blue shadows stretch beside them, filled with silver ice stars. The thief is long gone and they walk alone, suspended in a realm of ice and light, the city dissolved in the mist. Ruby feels the welcome warmth of the sun on her face and listens to the slowing thud of her heart. She has only taken a few steps into London and they have already come close to ruin. They still have to cross the city and find her father.

A crowd has gathered by the slipway, drawn by the excitement of the chase. Ruby jumps up onto Dervish's back and ties Molly on behind. Her hat is gone, lost in the ride through the winding lanes, so she pulls up the hood of her cloak and ties her scarf over her mouth to hide her face. At the foot of the slipway she draws her pistol.

The grim light in Ruby's eyes and the sight of her pistol is enough to keep the onlookers back and she rides past them without a word.

Ruby does not notice Mr. Famish, standing in a doorway at the foot of Darkhouse Lane. It takes a great deal to make Mr Famish leave the warmth of his den on a winter morning but he wants a first hand look at the girl who outwitted his whole gang. His eyes glisten with malice as Ruby passes.

"No doubt you think yourself a fine and clever lass," he mutters to himself. "But I'll have that horse off you, and I'll take your life too, if it pleases me. I don't like to be bested by anyone."

Ruby rides on, oblivious to the danger, with no idea that she is followed, every step of the way, by one of Mr. Famish's spies.

Chapter 2 - Hackney

Ruby rides out of the City, up Bishopsgate and out onto the Hackney Road. The city smoke falls away and the road winds on through the woods of Cambridge Heath, wrapped in pale morning mist. She does not see the ragged boy following her, hiding in the hedge each time she stops.

Jimmy Twig has sharp eyes and he is fast on his feet. He would prefer doorways to hide in but the mist is good enough. He keeps the rider in sight and stays as close to her as he dares. The road runs on over the Heath, taking him further and further from the rat alleys of the city. The sky out here is bigger than he is used to and the air is cleaner. It's exiting and more than a little terrifying.

Mr. Famish told him to follow and that's what he'll do, but Jimmy wonders how far the fierce eyed girl on the chestnut horse will go?

Ruby crosses the frozen marsh at the edge of the village and stops at the Inn on Meare Street to ask for directions. She rides up onto Church Street and a few minutes later she halts her horses by the gate of Hawkins' livery yard. Jimmy Twig is close behind. He finds a gap in the ivy covered wall opposite the yard and hunkers down to wait. He is hungry and cold but he dare not go back to Mr Famish until he has something to tell.

Seth Gilbert stands at the stable door, holding the bridle of a black coach horse while his daughter Katy grooms the animal with heavy bristle brush. The horse's coat is matted with dried mud and the brush sends up a fine dust as she works.

"Am I doing it right?" asks Katy.

"Watch his ears," said Seth. "If they're relaxed then you can guess that he likes what you're doing. If he's laid them back flat then you better watch out." He pats the horse's neck, running his hand over the glossy black coat. Seth is blind but he can tell the temper of a horse from the feel of it under his hand. "He seems happy to me. You keep up your brushing."

Ruby sits watching the man and the girl in the stable yard. Her father looks older that she remembers. His hair is silver grey and his face is lined with sorrow. Katy is a whole head taller than she was when Ruby last saw her and her expression is unusually serious as she works the brush through the coach horse's muddy coat. The change in her little sister brings Ruby up sharp.

It is seven months since her family sailed away from Cornwall, fleeing for their lives. For Ruby that time passed in the blink of an eye. She rode away from the beach with Davey on Midsummer's Eve and found a gate into the land of Faerie. The next thing she knew, it was half a year later and she was alone on the snow covered moor. Here in the wintery street, with carts going by, the whole thing seems like dream.

Ruby feels in her pocket for the golden leaf, the cool touch of it on her palm reassuring her that she did not imagine the whole thing.

Dervish gives a soft whinny and Seth turns his head. "Who's there?" he calls, his face alert. "I know that horse . . ."
Katy turns too. She gives a whoop of joy, drops the grooming brush and runs across the stable yard.
"It's Ruby! She's come back. I told you she would."
Ruby jumps down to grab her sister up in her arms and a moment later Seth is there too, hugging both of his daughters, with tears of joy in his unseeing eyes.
"It's good to have you back lass," he says. "You have Dervish with you. Where's Davey?"
Katy sees a cloud pass over her sister's face.
"He's far away . . ." Ruby begins. She stops, lost for words. She doesn't want to talk about that, not yet.
"I'll tell you soon enough but first I must see to Molly and Dervish. We've been riding for days and Dervish is hurt."

It is only when Dervish and Molly have been fed and installed in the stable and Dervish's wounds have been dressed, that Ruby feels able to tell her story. They are sitting by the fireplace in the cosy parlour of the livery stable while Seth's sister, Hannah, fusses about them, making tea and toasting bread over the fire on a long wire fork. Hannah and her husband, Sid Hawkins, have given the Gilbert's a new home after they fled Cornwall. Ruby's father is now head stableman at Hawkins Yard and Katy is his chief assistant.

"Where's Tom?" asks Ruby. She can't imagine her brother working at a livery stable; he couldn't ride a horse to save his life.

"Mr. Blake will have him hard at work," says Hannah, passing Ruby a thick slice of buttered toast. "Eat up. You look half starved."

"Tom'll be back soon," said Seth. "Unless he stops by the inn on his way from the printer's."

"He's a talented boy," says Hannah. "Mr Blake is lucky to have him as an apprentice. That picture above the hearth is one that he made."

Ruby looks up at the etching in a wooden frame over fireplace. It shows a tree filled valley overlooking the sea. In the foreground a carthorse ploughs furrows in a field beside a little cottage. Tom has drawn the view over Bascome Valley so well that Ruby knows it at once. She catches her breath as sudden tears prick at the back of her eyes.

"Tom always loved to draw when he was a boy," says Seth."I remember him sitting on the back steps of the cottage scratching away on a slate, making pictures of horses and flowers. He stopped all that after your mother left us."

Ruby nods, remembering how carefree Tom had been before their mother died.

Ruby was in Bascome only three weeks ago and she shudders to think of how changed the place is. The ruins of their burned out cottage had lain deep in snow and in the middle of the field had been a stone mill house for the new mine. An ugly road had been cut through Fiddler's wood and many of the trees had been felled. Ruby had found her hidden glade by the stream but the place was changed. She'd taken the bag of gold hidden in the hollow tree and left without looking back.

Her whole life had been lived in that valley, until last summer, when Squire Colby tore it apart.

"Where've you been all this time?" asks Seth. "We'd all but given up hope."

"What's today's date?" asks Ruby.

"It's the second of February."

"You missed Christmas!" says Katy.

Ruby sighs. She has to begin somewhere.

"You won't believe half of what I tell you," she says. "Sometimes I'm not sure I believe it myself."

Ruby tells how she and Davey rode away from the beach at Zone point and how they met with Squire Colby. She tells how, in the end, Ruby spared the Squire's life. Seth scowls at this news but he keeps his silence.

"We rode over the moors to Smith's Den and there . . ." Ruby falters. She takes a deep breath and carries on. "We stepped through the gates into the Twilight Land. Queen Mab was waiting for us. She enchanted Davey and took him away with her. I tried to call him back but he was lost." She turns to look at Seth. "All those stories you used to tell, about the land of Faerie; I never believed in them, not really. I loved to hear them but I thought they were just fanciful tales.

"But there is another world - I've seen it. I've seen the flickering stars of Faerie and the people who live there and it is more strange than any tale."

"And Davey is still there?" asks Seth softly.

"He had no choice," says Ruby. "He'd made a bargain with Queen Mab, in return for saving my life."

"Is he gone forever?" asks Katy in a whisper.

"Not many come back from the Twilight Land," says Seth.

"He may be saved," says Ruby. "I made a bargain of my own with Queen Mab. I pledged to return to the gates of Faerie at Midsummer and bring her a lost jewel from her crown. If I can't find it then Davey will be trapped in Faerie for good."

Ruby doesn't tell her father the other part of the bargain, that she will forfeit her own life if she fails to find Queen Mab's jewel.

Silence falls in the parlour. Katy stares up at her sister in wide eyed wonder, while Seth sits still and solemn. Hannah is staring too, the toast on her fork burning to ashes over the fire. The smell of burning bread wakes her from her trance and shakes he flaming crust into the hearth.

"You are as fanciful a story teller as your father ever was!" Hannah says. "I'll go and fetch more bread. Katy, I'm leaving you to try and talk some sense into your sister."

"Everything I've told you is true," says Ruby, once Hannah is gone.

"I've never stepped through the gates of Faerie," says Seth. "Nor have I met any of the folk who live there.

But I've never known you to lie, Ruby. If you say it is true then I believe you."

"What was Queen Mab like?" asks Katy in a whisper.

"She was beautiful and strange and terrible and cruel. I felt like she might give me a great a gift or snuff my life out like a candle at any moment."

"What is the jewel you have to find?"

"It was stolen from Queen Mab's crown long ago and hidden somewhere in the Waking World."

"I remember a tale about that," says Seth. "The seven starred crown was given to Queen Mab by Loki, the god of mischief, but he came and stole back the greatest of the diamonds."

"Where did he take it?" asks Ruby.

"Loki swam away from Faerie in the shape of a salmon, carrying the diamond in his mouth. He swam through a crack in the edge of the world but the journey back to waking took so long that by the time he had returned he hadn't the strength to take his own shape. As he lay gasping for breath in the river shallows Loki was caught in a fishing net. He only escaped by giving up the gem to the fisherman. What became of the diamond after that the story doesn't tell."

"I'm not sure that helps much," sighs Ruby. She yawns. The fire and the food have worked an enchantment of their own upon her and it is all that she can do to follow Hannah up the stairs and fall into bed.

    Jimmy Twig has crept out from his hiding place in the ivy to peer in through the parlour window. He is frozen to the bone but he has been standing there for more than an hour, watching the Gilbert family as they sit by the hearth. The fierce eyed girl and her little sister have gone and only the old man remains, his face turned to the fire.

A half eaten piece of toast lies on a plate by the hearth. The sight of it reminds Jimmy how hungry he is but it is a deeper need that keeps him standing there on tip-toe, his nose pressed to the window. He has no words for the longing he feels; a hunger for a home that he has never known, and a yearning for love and kindness.

A hand reaches up to close the curtain and Jimmy slips down out of sight. He creeps away from the house and sets off along Church Street, back toward London. He is so cold that he can hardly breathe and the air is like a knife in his throat. The feeling comes back into his arms and legs as he runs and the pain is so sudden and sharp that he cries out.

Being Mr. Famish's spy is all that Jimmy has ever known - so why does he feel like a traitor? If only he could keep the memory of the fireside to himself, to hold close, like a talisman. It would be something of his own, a true and warm thing to sustain him in the darkness. But Jimmy knows very well that he'll sell all he knows to Mr Famish, in return for a bowl of soup and place to sleep for his sister and himself.

Jimmy runs, wiping a tear from his cheek and hardening his heart against the night.

Chapter 3 - The Dark Tower

Lord Ruin raises his eyes from the icy flames and gazes out over the wasteland below the tower. Nothing moves upon the darkling plain and there is no sound, nor a hint of wind to stir the dust of centuries, lying deep and bitter in the hollows of the land. The only light is the faint glow from the flickering stars far away beyond the mountains.

Lord Ruin has not moved his hand in a hundred lifetimes of men but he moves it now, reaching for the hilt of the sword that lies across his knees. He has heard the sound of his name, whispered far off beyond the edge of the world.

Rousing from his trance, Lord Ruin opens his mouth wide and shrieks in a voice as sharp as steel on stone.
"Pestilence, Suffering, Blight and Misery - awake!"
Ruin's cry shivers the foundations of the dark tower, echoing over the wasteland to the Mountains of Grief. The cry reverberates in every hall, down to the furthest dungeon, deep in the cold earth where the lost souls tremble in their chains and cower back into the shadows.

Lord Ruin's call fades into the empty silence and the darkness hold's its breath.

There comes the distant clink of a key turning in a rusty lock. There comes a moaning and a sighing and the sound of metal shod feet scraping on stone.

The Furies have woken.

Chapter 4 - Gutter Lane

"Katy's been telling me all sorts of tales," says Tom, getting up from the his seat at the kitchen table to hug Ruby."It seems that you've become story spinner like our father."

"It's not stories," says Katy. "They're true."

Tom smiles and ruffles Katy's hair. He looks back at Ruby:

"Where have you been all this time?"

There is a look on Tom's face that Ruby has not seen before; stern but kind. The sort of look a loving older brother might give to a wayward younger sister. Tom is a year older than Ruby but back in Cornwall it was always Ruby who looked after the family.

When Ruby rode into Faerie on Midsummer's Eve six months passed in the blink of an eye. The time has gone much slower here and the country boy who Ruby knew has been replaced by a young city gent. Tom's dark wool coat is smart, if a little ink-stained, his boots are clean and he has cut his hair. He also looks as if he has taken to having baths once in a while. The change in Tom is unsettling but not unwelcome.

Tom listens to Ruby's tale without word and when she is done he takes her hand:

"You've been through a lot, I can see that. You've lost Davey and a grief like that can affect a person. Goodness knows, I was a trial to you after our mother died." Tom shrugs. "It's all very well to make up stories for Katy but you can't live in those tales forever. Hannah is worried about you and so am I."

"I believe you," says Katie, glaring fiercely at Tom. "And so does Dad."

Ruby winks at her sister.

"I'm mighty glad to have you back," says Tom. "We've made a new home here and I'll do all I can to help you settle in. It's not Bascome Valley but it's not bad, once you get used to it."

Ruby nods. She can't blame Tom for being doubtful; he has not ridden under the stars of Faerie, nor spoken with Queen Mab. Would Ruby have believed her own tale if she had heard it a few months ago?

"I intend to find Queen Mab's lost Jewel," Ruby says firmly. "Rescuing Davey is all that matters. You know London better than me. If you want to help then tell me where I would start looking for a rare and precious diamond."

"Headstrong as ever," laughs Tom. "The high class Jewellers are on Bond Street but if you're looking for something out of the ordinary there's a fellow I know who might be able to help." Tom grins, a flash of the wild country boy returning to his face. "I came across a few crooked characters when we first arrived in London. Charlie Angel hears most things that happen in the City and he owes me a favour." He takes a battered pocket watch from his waistcoat and clicks it open. "I'm making deliveries for Mr Blake this morning. Come along with me and I'll take you to meet Charlie."

An hour later Tom and Ruby are riding over Cambridge heath in Mr Blake's dog cart, pulled along by an amiable pony named Bramble. Ruby sits next to Tom on the front seat, with Mr Blake's prints in a box between them. Tom is doing a fair job of driving the buggy and Ruby resists the urge to take the reins and trot the pony a little faster.

London is an assault upon the senses, both fascinating and repellant. The air is thick with smoke and the gutters are filled with stinking filth. The roads are mostly mud and horse dung, crusted with ice. There are palaces and cathedrals and high terraces of white stone houses where silk dressed ladies are helped up into carriages by servants in golden coats. There are shops hung with bright coloured cloths and hats and dresses, carts filled with flowers, and women at the street corners with baskets of bread and vegetables balanced on their heads. There are jugglers, street entertainers and tented booths with signs for fortune tellers and herbal doctors.

The wider streets are full of life and colour but the narrow alleys are sinister, shadowed places. The ancient houses lean at odd angles and the doorways are dark. The people here are ragged and pale and the children have no shoes on their feet.

They ride past St Paul's cathedral and on toward Newgate Prison, where the air stinks of human filth and the streets are the most squalid that they have seen so far.

Tom draws the buggy up beside a tavern called the Eagle. There is already a horse tied there and two filthy urchins sitting on the wall watching it. The biggest of them jumps down from his perch and comes running up to them.

"A farthing to mind your horse, sir?" His face is pinched and pale and he shivers in a threadbare coat, several sizes too small.

"I'll give you both sixpence if you promise to look after the pony and fetch him some fresh feed," says Ruby.

The boy's mouth falls open and his comrade comes scampering over. Ruby hands each of the boys a sixpence and the smaller one runs off at once to get a bag of oats.

"You're supposed to pay them after they've done the job of guarding the horse," says Tom. "They'll be expecting more when we return."

"I don't mind that," says Ruby. "The money in my purse isn't mine. Jack Shadow took it and if we were back in Cornwall he'd be sharing it with the people who need it most."

"Keep your voice down," says Tom, glancing round nervously. "Even in London, people have heard of Jack Shadow."

"Really?" asks Ruby. "What are they saying?"

Tom takes his sister by the arm and pulls her into a side street. The houses lean above them, making the alley dark as a tunnel.

"They say that there's a highwayman down in Cornwall who cheated the noose by making a pact with the devil," says Tom. "When they tried to hang him the souls of the dead rose up out of the earth and carried him away on their backs."

"It is strange how stories change with the telling," says Ruby."Do they make any mention of the highwayman being a thirteen year old girl?"

"Be quiet!" hisses Tom. "There is still a price on your head."

"I suppose I should be glad that people think that Jack Shadow is a man," says Ruby.

"And you should keep a tighter grip on your purse strings," says Tom. "You have a kind heart, Ruby, and I love you for it, but if you carry on throwing money about you'll have every cutpurse in London creeping after us."

Ruby draws her pistol from her cloak.

"I can take care of pickpockets," she says.

"Put that away! No London Lady would carry a thing like that."

"I'm not sure I want to be a Lady" says Ruby. "I'm hardly dressed for it."

She wears a black cloak and men's riding clothes - cleaner now, thanks to Aunt Hannah. A hat and scarf are all that it would take for her to become a highwayman once again. "You could tell people that I'm your brother?" she says

"You're too pretty to be a boy," says Tom. "You'll fool no-one."

"I managed well enough when I was Jack Shadow."

"That was at night. You had a mask over your face and a pistol in your hand." Tom shakes his head in exasperation. "For now, you'll be my long lost sister, Jane, newly arrived from the country. I'll tell people that you are a simple and unfamiliar with city ways - which is quite true."

"Jane?"

"It's a common name," says Tom. "A good one to hide behind."

Ruby laughs. Tom really has grown up these last six months and she is glad to have him as an ally.

"I'll let you call me Jane," she says, punching her brother in the ribs. "But don't expect me to act simple."

Tom leads them deeper into the warren of filthy back streets. They pass a woman sitting slumped in a doorway, cradling a broken gin bottle in her lap. Her eyes are glazed and in the shadowed room behind her Ruby see rats scuttling over the floor. Somewhere in the darkness a baby whimpers.

Ruby pulls Tom to a halt and a skeletal dog appears at the woman's side and growls.

"Who's there?" calls a gruff male voice.

"Come on," says Tom, tugging Ruby after him. "Gutter lane is no place to hang about and stare."

They turn into a street so narrow that they have to walk in single file and Tom halts outside a ramshackle house with a sign above the door in the shape of a jug. A man dressed in a dirty coat lies sprawled full length across the threshold.

"Is he dead?" asks Ruby.

Tom gives the man a tap in the ribs with the toe of his boot. The man groans but he does not open his eyes. "Dead drunk."

"What is this place?" asks Ruby.

"Molly Gun's Gin Shop," says Tom.

As Tom leads them inside, Ruby puts her hand under her cloak and takes a tight grip on the pistol.

The dim interior of the shop smells of rot and piss and sour gin. It is a low ceilinged cellar, lit by a pair of lanterns set on a trestle table that serves as a bar.

The floor is strewn with broken glass, and rats skitter in the corners.

It is not yet lunchtime but the occupants of Molly Gun's Gin Shop all seem to have had more then enough to drink. They sit propped up on chairs or slumped over the filthy tables in much the same state as the man at the door. An old man raises his glass to Ruby and begins to sing.

"Sin is heavier than the lead
and blessing is better than the bread
The wind is longer than the way
and love is deeper than the sea-"

He throws his arms out and falls off his chair with a crash.

"Do you spend much time in places like this?" asks Ruby.

"I wouldn't drink in here if you paid me. But it is where Charlie Angel is most likely to be found."

Behind the bar, a sour faced woman in a dirty apron looks up from the glass she is attempting to clean with a filth crusted rag. She fixes them with a malevolent glare and opens her mouth to speak but is distracted by a monkey dressed a bright green waistcoat, who jumps up onto the counter, bares its teeth and hisses at Ruby and Tom. The woman makes grab for the monkey but it scampers off along the bar, upsetting a row of metal flagons onto the floor.

"Come 'ere Judas, you little ratbag," yells Molly Gunn "I'll chain you up again, you see if I don't."

The monkey leaps onto a nearby table, grabs up a handful of broken walnut shells and begins throwing them at Molly Gunn with great enthusiasm and accuracy.

Tom steers Ruby toward the shadows at the back of the room and a line of wooden booths with long benches and tables. Most of the booths are empty but at the far end two men are hunched over a candle, deep in conversation.

The men turn as Ruby and Tom approach. The nearer one is a red cheeked boy of fourteen, with a tousled mess of pale blonde hair. He wears a tatty yellow frock coat and a beaming smile. The other man is older and narrow faced, with thinning grey hair and unfriendly eyes. At the sight of Ruby he appears utterly startled. He regains his composure almost at once and his stunned look is replaced with a scowl.

"I'll see you later," he mutters to the yellow coated boy. "Remember to keep your trap shut."

The thin faced man darts Ruby a spiteful look, grabs up his tobacco pouch from the table, and slides out of the booth. Ruby notices the man's fingernails, long and yellow, curved and sharpened into vicious points.

As the thin man stalks off into the shadows the boy hurriedly puts something away in his pocket. He turns to them and grins.

"Who have you brought with you, Tom?" he says. "We don't get many pretty girls in this place."

"This my sister, Jane," says Tom. "She's new in London, so you mind your manners"

"I am a gentleman, Tom, you know that," says Charlie, making a bow to Ruby. "Can I get you and your pretty sister a drink?"

Tom shakes his head:

"Molly Gunn's gin is worse than the stuff we use to clean the etching press. It'll rot your brain if you're not careful."

"That's true enough," says Charlie, winking at Ruby. "But Molly has some finer stuff she keeps under the counter for her regulars."

"I'm not thirsty," Ruby says. She is beginning to wish that she had never agreed to come and meet Charlie Angel.

"Sit down," says Charlie, gesturing to the benches. "How can I help you? Do you want me to give your sister a tour of the sights of London or are you thinking of giving up your honest trade and becoming a gentleman thief like me?"

"We're looking for something," says Tom. "I thought you might be able to help."

"It's a diamond," Ruby says. "A rare and special one."

"You've come to the right place," laughs Charlie. "We've nothing but rare diamonds here. Why, this very morning I heard of a gentleman who -"

There is sharp cough from somewhere nearby and Charlie stops in his tracks, the smile fading from his lips. Ruby looks around for the source of the sound but the only person in sight is a ragged man in a sailor's jacket, snoring face down at the next table. She spies a curl of white smoke rising from the next booth and guesses that the thin faced man is listening there.

"Tell me more about your diamond," asks Charlie, beaming once more."Was it lost? Was it stolen? Is there a reward for its return?"

"What makes you think we can trust him?" Ruby asks Tom.

"My dear Jane!" says Charlie. "I am as honest as day is long and I am most hurt by your insinuations."

"You told us yourself that you are a thief."

"Which just goes to show what an honourable fellow I am." Charlie smiles winningly. "A common pickpocket would have lied to you, but I am a man of honour."

"What about your friend in the next booth?"

A flicker of something like fear passes over Charlie's Face but his smile returns almost at once. He leans forward and whispers to Ruby.

"Don't mind him. I'll do all I can to help you, Jane. I'll gladly repay my debt to Tom by finding your lost gem."

Ruby whispers back:

"The jewel is not mine. I don't know of it is even in London. All that I know is it is a large diamond, the size of a hen's egg. It is clear and flawless and very old. I have to find it and return it to its owner in order to save someones life."

"What a tale!" laughs Charlie.

"I'll pay a fair price for any information," says Ruby evenly. "But if you try and cheat me you will regret it."

"Your sister is an original, 'aint she!" says Charlie. "I think I'm beginning to like her." He reaches for Ruby's hand. "There is no need to pay me, Jane." He takes a furtive look about and leans close again. "Best not say any more - this place is full of rogues - but if I hear any news of your jewel then I'll send word to Tom. All I ask in return is that you consider allowing me the honour of escorting you to the Vauxhall Gardens one afternoon. It is a most pleasant place for a stroll."

"My sister will have a chaperone if she goes anywhere with you," says Tom.

Charlie grins at Ruby.

"Is it a deal?"

"If you can find the diamond," she says.

"Why does Charlie Angel owe you a favour?" Ruby asks Tom, as they head back down Gutter Lane.

"I helped him out of a scrape. He was being chased by a gang of villains and I saved his skin by hiding him in the back of Mr Blake's wagon."

"Charlie's a bit of a villain himself," says Ruby. "Are you sure he hadn't robbed them?"

"I didn't ask," Tom shrugs. "But I reckon Charlie's alright. Anyway, it's not long since you were a Highwayman."

"He knew more than he told us," says Ruby.

The booth behind Charlie Angel had been empty when they'd stepped out to leave Molly Gun's but the smell of pipe tobacco still hung in the air. Ruby's instincts tell her that the thin faced man is dangerous. As for Charlie Angel; she doubts if he will be able to find the diamond.

Jimmy Twigg slips out from his hiding place behind the barrel, steps over a snoring drunk and runs to the door in time to peer after Ruby and Tom hurrying away down the alley. Why would she be meeting with one of Mr Famish's thieves? It makes no sense.

Jimmy creeps back along the bar toward the back of the gin shop. Mr Famish has rejoined Charlie Angel in the booth and they are leaning close and whispering. Jimmy moves closer, his heart pounding.

"It sounds like the same jewel," says Charlie. "The one that the other fellow was after."

"An interesting coincidence," replies Mr. Famish.

"If we can find the diamond then we can sell it twice over and double our money."

"Any money will be mine, whelp. You'll get a cut if you follow orders."

Charlie looks petulant.

"If it's to be that way then perhaps I'll just help Jane Gilbert myself and -"

"Was that the name she gave you?" snarls Mr Famish. "You always were a dolt, Charlie Cobb - ever since you were my errand boy."

"I'm my own man now," says Charlie

Famish smiles and it is such an ugly thing to see that Charlie wishes he would go back to scowling.

"You'll always be one of my boys. You bear the mark of my whip and you'll never forget where your loyalties lie."

Charlie turns as pale as chalk.

"You'll do as I tell you," says Mr. Famish. "Find out all you can about the blessed diamond. I don't know the game Miss Gilbert is playing but I will get to the heart of it. I smell gold in this."

Mr Famish's eyes narrow. He shoots out his arm and drags Jimmy to him with a hiss of rage.

"What are you up to?"

"I was following her, like you said," stammers Jimmy Twigg. "Ruby Gilbert was in here, sitting right at this table with Charlie."

"I know that, you vermin," spits Famish. He slams Jimmy's head down onto the table and presses a knife to his throat. He leans over Jimmy and whispers in his ear. "If I catch you spying on me again I will slit your throat and throw your flea bitten carcass in the river. Understand?" Jimmy nods, his eyes wide with terror. Famish throws Jimmy to the floor and gives him a kick. "Get after her, before I snap you in two."

Chapter 5 - Eel pies

The next morning Ruby rides back into the city alone. She has a map in her pocket, sketched by Tom onto the back of an old playbill.

She walks the length of Bond Street, stopping at every jeweller's shop, but none of them have heard of Queen Mab's diamond. By the time she reaches Oxford Street her boots are filthy and her clothes are spattered with mud from the passing carriages. At the last shop the doorman takes one look at her and shakes his head.

"This is a high class place," he says. "No riffraff." The shop is grander than the others, with a mirrored glass sign over the door proclaiming the place to be *Maison Lucien*. The cold eyed doorman is giant of a fellow, dressed in a spotless red and gold uniform and white gloves.

"My money is as good as anyone else's," says Ruby. The doorman leans down and Ruby feels the heat of his sour breath on her face.

"On your way, malkintrash," he whispers, putting up his huge fist. "Don't make me dirty my gloves by throwing you into the street."

Ruby turns away, fuming. She hauls herself up on Molly's back and is about to ride off when a carriage comes to a halt at the curb, blocking her way.

The carriage is drawn by four white horses with silver bridles and there is golden crest painted onto the door. Ruby stares in wonder as a pair of yellow coated footmen leap from the back of the carriage and unroll a length of carpet over the paving stones, making a mud free path to the shop door. They step to one side and a lady in a blue silk dress steps down. Her face is painted white and her silvery wig is piled high on her head. Two maids follow, dressed in green, one of them carrying a small white dog with a diamond encrusted collar.

"Lady Winter!" says the doorman. He bows low and opens the door of Maison Lucien. Lady Winter walks past without any acknowledgement but the second maid lets fall some coins. She drops them quite deliberately, just out of the doorman's reach, and giggles as he falls to his knees to scrabble for the fallen pennies on the pavement. The maid turns to glance back at the footmen, her eyes the same acid shade of green as her dress. The footmen smirk and exchange a laugh at the doorman's expense.

"What a sorry lot you are," says Ruby. She knows that it would be better to hold her tongue but she can't help herself. "Each one of you thinking you are better than the other. Truth is - you are nothing but beggars dressed up in fancy rags."

The green eyed maid gives Ruby a poisonous look, the footmen stop laughing and the doorman glares up at her, red faced with rage and humiliation.

Ruby urges Molly on and rides away up Oxford Street. The doorman yells after her but his shout is lost under the clatter of Molly's hooves on the cobblestones.

Ruby rides up to Hatton Garden and on to Gold Street. The diamond merchants and goldsmiths are more friendly than the snobbish shopkeepers on

Bond Street but they have not heard of Queen Mab's diamond.

On Cheapside Ruby catches the smell of food.
"Eely pies - hot, hot, hot!" Comes a cry. She looks down to see an aged woman sitting on a stool beside a cloth covered barrow. On the back of the barrow stands a little girl of about six years old, yelling at the top of her voice.
"Juniper's pies. The best in London. Only a Penny each!"

Ruby brings Molly to a halt.
"I've never had an eel pie before," she says.
"Never ate one of Grannie Juniper's pies?" laughs the old woman."You ain't lived." She turns to the little girl. "Lilly, fetch the Lady a nice hot one."
Lilly dives down under the cloth and comes up with a steaming hot pie in her hands. Ruby climbs down from Molly's back and gives a penny to Grannie Juniper. The pie crust is golden brown, with a shining glaze, and when she bites into it the inside is sweet and salty and wonderful.
"This is good," says Ruby, wiping gravy from her chin.
"Didn't I say they was the best in London?" laughs Grannie Juniper.

The pie turns to ashes in Ruby's mouth when she sees him. The boy is doing his best to stay in the shadows but the doorway he has chosen is too shallow to hide him. Ruby has noticed him a couple of times already, outside the diamond merchants on Hatton Garden and again on Gold Street. She has a suspicion that he's been following her all day.

The boy is so thin that its hard to be sure how old he is. He's the same height as Lilly Juniper but his eyes are older. The sharp angles of his bones show through his ragged clothes, he is pale and filthy and there is a livid bruise on his cheek. He presses himself back into the door frame like a baby rabbit, hunching down in the grass to hide from a hunting hawk.

There are so many starving children in London. Lilly Juniper is one of the lucky ones; she has to work hard but she has enough to eat and has at least one person who cares for her. Who does this boy have?

Ruby has known her share of poverty - she suffered it herself in Cornwall - but the poverty in the city is different. Winter in the countryside can be cruel but the rest of the year even the most destitute country person can glean a meal from the hedgerow. There are rabbits to snare and clean water to drink. And when your belly is empty there is beauty to feast upon, the sky above you and the clean wind in your hair. In London the poor are crammed together like beasts in a great filthy cage. And there are so many of them, so many thin faced children that it breaks Ruby's heart.

The most maddening thing is that rich are here too, cheek to cheek with ragged and the hopeless, gadding about in their fine carriages, stepping over beggars as they make their way along the streets. The roofs of the slums are visible from the high white houses and they can smell the stink of them when the wind blows in the wrong direction. How can they let things carry on this way?

The injustice of it makes Ruby so angry that she can hardly breathe.

She crosses the street and holds the pie out the boy. His eyes widen but he makes no move to take it.

"It's good," she says. "The best pie in London."

The boy looks up at Ruby; wary, fearful and hopeful. He looks at the pie and slowly puts out his grubby hands to take it. He pulls his arms back, holds the pie to his chest, then turns to run, leaping past Ruby and away up the street.

"You've a kind heart," says Grannie Juniper, when Ruby goes back to buy another pie. "The world would be a better place if there was more folk like you."

Lilly is watching Ruby thoughtfully from her perch on the back of the barrow.

"Don't stand there gawping, Lil," laughs Grannie Juniper. "Fetch the lady her pie."

Lilly gets Ruby her lunch then jumps back up onto the barrow to shout again:

"Eely pies. Eely pies oh! Hot, hot, hot!"

Jimmy Twig watches Ruby from his hiding place behind a cart. He sits on the frozen cobbles, stuffing the wonderful pie into his face as fast as he can. Just in time, he remembers to save a bit for Rosie. Less than half the pie remains but it's a big enough piece. He slips it into his pocket, as carefully as if it were treasure.

Jimmy is careful not to let Ruby catch sight of him again. He follows her along Cheapside and onto Lombard Street. She stops at several goldsmith's and jeweller's shops but she doesn't seem to find what she is looking for. At last, she heads for home, despondent.

Chapter 6 - The Wolf at the Well

Ruby hears the shrieking of the horses from half way down Church Street. She nudges Molly on towards Hawkins yard but before she reaches the gate someone steps out from the shadows and puts a hand to her stirrup. It is a ragged girl with a wild tangle of hair, a year or so younger than Ruby, dressed in a shapeless grey dress, a muddy pinafore and an oversized pair of men's boots.

"Please, Miss Ruby," says the girl. "I need to speak to you -"

Molly gives a shudder of terror and rears back in panic.

"Steady girl," says Ruby, putting hand on Molly's neck. The grey horse sets her feet down but she refuses to be calmed. She rolls her eyes and skitters sideways, seemingly desperate to get away from the ragged girl.

The girl backs away, tears starting in her eyes.

"I'm sorry," she says. "I can't help it."

"It's no your fault that my horse is moonstruck," says Ruby. "I don't know what's got into her."

Inside Hawkins Yard the rest of the horses are working themselves into a frenzy, kicking at the stall doors and screaming.

"What's happening in there?"

"I best go," says the wild haired girl. "I don't mean to bring trouble but it follows wherever I go." She backs away and points down the lane "There's a well, down by the willow tree. Please, Miss Ruby, meet me there. It's important-"

"How do you know my name?" asks Ruby.
But the girl is gone, running around the corner and up the lane.

Ruby leans down to whisper to Molly, her free hand reaching for the charm around her neck. A galloping horse in a battered circle of bronze, the Kern holds deep magic. Ruby calls upon the Kern's power to calm Molly and the grey horse soon settles.

"Something scared them horses silly," Ruby says, as she jumps down from Molly's back. "What was it?"
Sid Hawkins shrugs:
"I chased off some nag runners from the gate last night," he says." They might have come back."
The ragged girl hadn't seemed much like a horse thief. She'd been scared stiff. Her accent was Cornish and she'd known Ruby's name. What was she doing here?

Ruby unsaddles Molly, settles her in her stall and heads off to find out more.

A sparrow bobs along the frozen lane, past hedges flecked with gold in the setting sun. The bird heads to the well and lands on the wooden trestle that supports the bucket on its iron chain.

The ragged girl is waiting by the old willow tree. Her eyes are fierce and strange, more like the eyes of a wild animal. Her face is pale and her cheeks are scratched, as if she is in the habit of crawling through hedges. Her black hair is tangled with bits of broken twig and her clothes look as if they belong to several different people, all of them larger than she is.

"Who are you?" asks Ruby.

"Lucy Cotton, Miss." The wild girl frowns. "At least, that was my name. I'm not really sure who I am now."

Lucy Cotton? The name chimes in Ruby's memory. "You were the kitchen maid at Colby Hall?"

"I ran away." For all her fierceness Lucy Cotton suddenly looks as if she might cry.

"It's alright," says Ruby, putting a hand on Lucy's arm.

"I didn't come to talk about my troubles," says Lucy. "I came to warn you. The diamond that you are searching for - the one that Queen Mab lost from her crown - it has a curse on it . . ." Lucy stammers to a halt, then shakes herself. "Loki stole the jewel from her but when he swam back to the waking world he had to give it up to win his freedom. "A chill shiver runs down Ruby's spine. She has heard this story from Seth already but something about the way that Lucy tells it makes it seem far more real. "When Loki gave up the diamond he put a curse on it," says Lucy. "Anyone who owns it is doomed to die a terrible death."

"Who told you this?" asks Ruby.

"It was Queen Mab's servants. I heard them laughing about it after she sent you away. They thought it was funny - how you had been sent off on a quest to find a cursed gem and how you would soon be dead, either way." Lucy scowls and her eyes spark wth rage."They were a spiteful pair, dressed in magpie's feathers and ratty black fur. They called Mab's diamond the Faerie

Star and they said that Loki's curse is the reason that it has been lost for so long."

"You have been to Faerie?" asks Ruby in a whisper.

"I followed you and Davey," says Lucy. "Davey saved me when I was lost on the moors, that first night, and I want to help him as much as you do."

The quiet is shattered by a sudden whinny of terror and they turn to see a man attempting to lead a mule cart up the track towards the well. The mule is kicking and screaming, pulling at its harness, while the driver struggles to keep it from bolting. The man's dog is a few feet ahead of him, crouched low on the ground, its hackles raised, staring straight at Lucy. The dog gives a bark, turns tail and runs.

"Scamp, you daft mutt. Come back here!" shouts the mule driver.

The dog runs faster, howling as it goes, and the maddened mule manages to pull itself free from the driver's grasp.

  Lucy turns to look at the sky. The sun has set and the moon is silvering the horizon.

"I have to go," says Lucy. "You'll have to find another way to save Davey. The Faerie Star is deadly."

Lucy's voice is drowned out by the braying of the crazed mule as it tries to drag the cart through the hedge.

"Do not follow me, " shouts Lucy, her eyes wild with sudden fury. "The moon is coming! I'll do all I can to help you. Ragwort has promised to aid you as well."

"Who is Ragwort?"

Ruby gets no answer; Lucy Cotton is already running away down the track into the trees.

Jimmy Twig watches Ruby as she helps the mule driver. The Mule calms at Ruby's touch and the two of them haul the cart out of the hedge. The little dog comes slinking back and winds itself round Ruby's ankles. She scratches it behind the ears and heads off down the lane to Hawkins Yard.

All that Jimmy caught of the conversation beside the well was the word "Diamond". The beggar girl knows something about it and Mr Famish will reward Jimmy if he can find out more. He leaves Ruby and follows the path that the other girl took, along the path past the old willow tree. The sun is gone but there's enough of a glow left in the sky to show the way ahead.

The track winds between hawthorn hedges. There are gates from time to time but the fields beyond are empty. Jimmy presses on, running as fast as he can, following the track into a copse of birch trees.

The moon is coming up fast, making it easier to see the path. Jimmy turns a corner by a fallen oak tree and stops in his tracks.

A ragged shape looms up. The wolf's fur glistens silver grey in the moonlight and its teeth are as white as death. Jimmy looks into the great beasts yellow eyes and gives a whimper of terror. The wolf lowers its snout and growls.

Jimmy runs. He runs as he has never run in his life, his feet leaping under him like birds, his screams echoing over the fields all the way to Shoreditch. He runs back along the track, feeling the wolf's breath on his neck, hearing the clash of its terrible teeth. He runs past the well and the willow tree, down the lane towards the only safe place he can think of. He scrambles over the gate of Hawkins yard in a heartbeat, jumps down the other side and runs up the hayloft ladder like a shadow. He dives down behind a pile of hay bales and lies shivering in the dusty darkness, his ears pricked for the slightest sound.

Jimmy Twigg hears no following footsteps, only the clatter of a cart on the cobbles down on Church Street. He hears the horses moving below him in their stalls, the scuffle of a mouse and the sigh of the wind in the roof. And then, far off in the night, he hears a rising howl that turns his blood to ice. He burrows down under the hay and lies there, as still and silent as a stone.

Chapter 7 - Jimmy Twigg

Sunlight slants down through the hayloft window onto Ruby's face. She wraps her cloak more tightly about her. It is cold up here, despite the sun, but it's a good place to consider her next move.

She has no doubt that the tale Lucy Cotton told was true; the fact that she knew about Ruby and Davey's journey into Faerie is enough to convince her of that. She wonders what Davey is doing now? Is he sitting at Queen Mab's feet with those other enchanted ones, with no memory of his waking life? Even if Ruby can succeed in her task what will be left of Davey after his time in Faerie? The stories agree that no-one returns from the Twilight Land unchanged.

Knowing that the diamond is cursed is not all bad; a jewel bearing a deadly curse is sure to leave some mark upon the world. There will be tales of it. Ruby just has to find them.

A sparrow flutters in at the window and comes to land on the hay beside Ruby's hand. It looks up at her, a bright fleck of sunlight catching in its dark eye. Ruby remembers the sparrow that came to her in her cell as she waited to be taken to the gallows.
"I survived that," says Ruby. "I'll find my way out of this."
The sparrow bobs its head and spreads its wings. It flies upwards, swooping in and out of the rays of sunlight. It begins to circle, its wings beating more swiftly than Ruby has ever seen a sparrow's wings move before. She watches in wonder as the bird flies faster still, swirling about until its flight becomes a

blur, scattering fragments of light like golden sparks onto the hay. The hay trembles and Ruby imagines that it might be about to catch fire, but what happens next is far stranger:

Green blades of grass rise from the dry hay, they twist and unfurl and stand straight. Leaves appear and budding stalks come spiralling up. The leaves spread and the buds open out into poppies, cornflowers and bright yellow buttercups.

The sparrow slows and takes shape once more out of the haze of light. It swoops down and lands on the hay beside the patch of summer flowers, puts its head on one side and looks at Ruby.

"You are no ordinary bird," whispers Ruby.

The sparrow nods its head.

Ruby knows what Faerie magic can do but the sight of summer flowers blooming in the hayloft of Hawkins Yard is the most wonderful thing that she has ever seen. She remembers what Lucy Cotton said, just before she ran into the night.

"Are you Ragwort?" Ruby asks in a hushed whisper

The sparrow lifts it wings and beats them in the air, chirruping loudly.

"Lucy said that you would come to help me."

The little bird takes to the air, fluttering over to the hayloft ladder where it lands and turns back to look at Ruby.

"You want me to follow?" she asks.

The sparrow nods its head.

There is a sudden scuffling in the corner of the hayloft. The noise is too loud for a rat and Ruby grabs up the nearby pitch fork.

"Who's there?"

"Please - don't kill me," comes a frightened voice."I don't mean no harm."

A scrap of shadow detaches itself from the wall and comes slowly out into the light. It is the beggar boy who Ruby gave the eel pie to on Cheapside. He is even grubbier than last time she saw him and covered from head to foot in straw.

"You followed me home?"

The boy nods, his eyes fixed on the prongs of Ruby's pitch fork. Ruby lowers the fork and sets it down. She glances over at the ladder where the sparrow waits patiently for her to follow.

The boy is staring at the patch of wildflowers growing in the hay.

"You can do magic," he says, looking to Ruby with wide eyes.

"It wasn't me," says Ruby, nodding to the sparrow.

"I saw you make the flowers grow," says the boy. "Are you an enchantress?"

The boy offers no obvious threat but Ruby senses danger in him, nevertheless. Why is he here? Did he follow her all the way from the city? The wary glint in his eye tells her that he is unlikely to give her a straight answer.

Ruby makes her face as fierce as she can:
"You've discovered my secret," she says. "But you must be careful. I will turn you into a frog if you displease me."

The boy blinks in terror. Ruby feels a pang of guilt but she presses on. "Answer my questions truthfully and you have nothing to fear."

The boy nods.

"Why did you follow me?"

"Mr. Famish told me to," says the boy. "He said I was to stick to you like a flea on a dog's arse and tell him everything that you do."

"Who is Mr. Famish and why is he interested in me?" Jimmy considers his answer. Mr Famish will whip him if he finds out that he has talked to Ruby Gilbert. But Ruby is everything that Mr Famish is not. She is kind and brave. She gave him wonderful eel pie to eat and she can do magic.

"Mr. Famish is after the diamond - same as you. I'm supposed to watch you and see if you find it."

"What have you told him about me?"

"I ain't told him nuffink since yesterday," says Jimmy."Before then I just told him where you live and who is here guarding the horses. That was all I knew then."

"What do you know now?"

"The diamond is in London," says Jimmy.

"Mr Famish says that some other gent is looking for it too." He looks down at the flowers. "Can I touch them?"

Ruby nods.

The little boy puts down his hand to stroke the green stems and his pinched, frightened face seems to light up from the inside.

"They're real," he says, looking up at her in even greater wonder. "I thought it might be a trick."

"What's your name?" asks Ruby.

"Jimmy Twigg," says the boy, touching his fingertip to the soft red petals of a poppy.

"Does Mr Famish often ask you to spy on people?"

"I'm one of Famish's boys. I do whatever he tells me." Jimmy frowns, his fear of his master getting the better of him. "I shouldn't say no more. I shouldn't've told you what I already done. Mr Famish would kill me if he knew."

"I'll not tell him," says Ruby. "Did Mr Famish give you the bruise on your cheek?"

Jimmy Twigg's face closes up and his eyes turn dark. "I ain't saying nuffink," he says. He glances over at the ladder, clearly figuring out his escape route. He sees the sparrow sitting there and thinks better of it. If Ruby is a witch then the bird might be magic too, like a witch's cat.

"Does Mr. Famish feed you, Jimmy?" asks Ruby.

"Sometimes," Jimmy shrugs. "If I do as he says."

"What about your parents?"

"Mr Famish is all I got," says Jimmy.

"You don't have to go back to him, you know. My uncle owns this yard. He needs a stable boy. I could talk to him about taking you on."

"I couldn't do that," says Jimmy. "Mr Famish would come for me. I'm his boy. He owns me like you own your horse."

"People can't own each other," says Ruby.

But this is not true; Jimmy Twigg is bound to Mr Famish as surely as any slave, chained by fear. It will take more than a few kind words and an eel pie to change that.

"I can't leave Rosie," says Jimmy. "She wouldn't last a day without me."

"Who's Rosie?"

"My sister."

"She could come too."

"Mr Famish won't let her go - not never. He calls her his Golden Key."

"Why?"

"She's the same age as me but she's littler and prettier. They leave her on a doorstep all wrapped up in a blanket and the people in the house take pity on her and carry her inside and then in the night she sneaks down and opens the window and Famish's men come and rob everything."

"That's an evil thing to do," says Ruby. "To take advantage of people's kind hearts."

"Mr. Famish doesn't have a heart."

"Next time Rosie is left on a doorstep the two of you must come straight here."

"Mr Famish would know," says Jimmy. "He knows everything. He'd find us and burn this place down. He'd take Rosie back and lock her up and he'd throw me in the river to drown."

"I'm not afraid of Mr Famish," says Ruby

"You should be, Miss," says Jimmy. "Mr. Famish is the devil."

Ruby can see the fear in Jimmy's eyes.

"You go back to Mr Famish tell him that I am a royal terror," says Ruby. "Tell him that I am a crack shot with a pistol and he will regret the day he crosses me."

"I ain't sayin' that," says Jimmy, smiling shyly. "Mr Famish would eat me alive."

Ruby reaches into her cloak and takes out her purse. She hands Jimmy a sixpence.

"From now on you shall have two masters," she says. "You can follow me all you like but I shall be the one to decide what you tell Mr Famish - do you agree?" Jimmy looks down at the silver coin and back up at Ruby, his terror of Mr Famish struggling with his awe of Ruby.

"If you do as I ask then I shall pay you well," says Ruby. She tries to make her face as fierce as she can. "But if you say a word of it to Mr Famish I'll know and I will use my magic on you."

Ruby hates to scare Jimmy but she needs to be certain that he will hold his tongue, for his own sake as much as hers.

"Can I take a flower for Rosie?" asks Jimmy.

Ruby bends down and picks the wildflowers from the hay. She ties them into a bunch with a bit of twine and hands him the posy.

"You go back to Mr Famish and tell him I went to every jeweller in London. Tell him that I found no trace of the diamond. And then you tell him that you heard me say that I'm so desperate that I'm off to Covent Garden to consult a fortune teller."

"You shouldn't waste your money," says Jimmy. "They're all cheats."

"I'm not going near a fortune teller," laughs Ruby. "But it should keep Mr Famish off my trail for a bit."

Jimmy nods and puts the sixpence away in his pocket.

"Yes, Miss."

"My name is Ruby."

"Yes, Miss Ruby."

Ruby watches from the hayloft window as Jimmy Twigg scampers away along Church Street. When she is certain that he is gone, she turns back to the sparrow. The little bird has perched up in the rafters but when it sees that Ruby is ready it flaps down to the top of the ladder again.

"All right," says Ruby. "Where are we going?"

Chapter 8 - Sparrow Path.

Ruby follows the sparrow out of the yard and along the lane towards the well. The bird darts into the hedge behind the willow tree, where Ruby finds a narrow gap between the thorny stems. The sparrow leads her on, past a field of frozen turnips and over a plank bridge across a ditch of icy water. The sparrow's flight winds onwards through the fields and woods until Ruby is quite lost. They cut across the roads and go by way of animal tracks and paths made by children, hidden from view by hedges and crumbling fences. They cross Finsbury Fields, pass Frog Hall, and head down towards Clerkenwell. They see no-one and they hear no-one, moving on the edge of the world, in a realm of shadows and secrets.

They come to the city and the sparrow flutters into an alley behind the shabby houses on Rag Street. Amid the crowds on Saffron Hill, Ruby does her best to look as if she knows where she is heading, the sparrow bobbing along ahead, perching on shop signs and windowsills to wait for her to catch up.

After a time, they come to places that Ruby has seen before. She hurries down Gutter Lane with her hood pulled over her face, wishing that she had her pistol with her. No-one notices the sparrow lofting up over Cheapside, nor pays any attention to Ruby as she heads past Grannie Juniper's pie barrow on the corner of Bread Street, where Lilly is as hard at work as ever, shouting her head off.

"Eely pies! Eelly pies - oh! The best in London!"

The sparrow swoops down into Star Alley and comes to rest on a brightly painted shop sign in the shape of a red and golden bird. Below the sign hang three golden balls, marking the shop out as a pawnbroker's. Behind the dusty glass of the shop window are bits of cheap jewellery and old china ornaments.

"Here?" Ruby asks.

The sparrow nods his head.

There is a small wooden sign fixed to the door of the shop. The gold paint is peeling away but Ruby can just about make out the words:

Solomon Phoenix - Pawnbroker, Diviner and Astrologer.

She looks up again at the sparrow.

"Are you sure?"

The bird gives an impatient chirrup and flaps its wings. Ruby shrugs and pushes open the door.

The interior of the shop is dim and smells of woodsmoke and spices, mixed with the stink of rotten eggs and the hot scent of a forge. The only light comes from the dirty shop window. By its faint illumination Ruby can make out a wooden counter with a collection of glass bottles arranged upon it. Behind the counter is a black velvet curtain and marble statue of a slim boy with curling hair and winged feet. The expression on the stone face is amused and wise, reminding Ruby of Queen Mab's enigmatic messenger, Perian.

There is no sign of the shopkeeper.

"Hello," Ruby calls out. "Is there anyone home?"

There is a crash of shattering glass and muffled curse from behind the curtain, followed by the shuffle of feet. The curtain is pushed aside and an old man appears. He is dressed in a grubby brown robe and dark blue Turkish slippers, curling up at the toes. His white hair is tangled like a bird's nest and his long beard is knotted and stained with splashes of green and yellow. The man's blue eyes are as sharp as steel and he does not look in the least pleased to see her.

"If you want a love potion then you have come to wrong place," the old man says. "Madame Isis's shop is on Friday Street. You can't miss it. There is a large stuffed crocodile in the window."

"I didn't come for a potion," says Ruby.

The man gives her a weary look.

"What do you wish to pawn?" he asks.

"No sir, not that either," Ruby is suddenly at a loss as to what to say. She has followed the sparrow hoping for some clue about the lost diamond. Has it all been for nothing?

Ruby catches the bitter smell of burning hair. A thin curl of smoke rises from the old man's robe and a red patch smoulders on the sleeve of his robe.

"You seem to be on fire," says Ruby.

The man scowls and glances down at his arm.

"Suffering salamanders!" He begins to beat at the sleeves of his robe with his hand but this only seems to fan the fire and a yellow flame crackles up at the end of his beard.

Ruby grabs up the nearest bottle from the counter and pulls off the top.

"Hold still!" she shouts, pouring the entire contents over the man's beard and arm. The flames hiss out in a cloud of steam.

The old man stares at his scorched sleeve and sighs. From the several other burnt patches on his robe it is clearly not the first time that he has set fire to himself.

"I hope this wasn't too expensive," said Ruby, holding up the empty bottle. "It seemed the best thing to do ..."

The man looks up. His face is still set in a scowl but there is glitter of amusement in his eyes.

"I am very much obliged to you, young lady," he says. "Without your intervention I might have combusted entirely." He takes the bottle from Ruby and peers at the label. "Lachrimae Angelus - Angels Tears." He gives Ruby a wink. "The perfect antidote to the fires of hell." He smiles. "To tell the truth, there was nothing in the bottle but spring water from the Maiden's Well. Such trickery is a debasement of my art but I have to keep body and soul together somehow."

There is a loud chirrup and the old man turns to see the sparrow, perched on the head of the statue. He stares hard at the bird then looks back at Ruby.

"The bird is accompanying you, I take it?"

"Yes," says Ruby. "It led me here. I'm not sure why"

"Most interesting." The old man blinks and smiles at Ruby. "Let us see if we can find out why you are here. Allow me to introduce myself." He makes a stiff bow. "I am Solomon Phoenix."

"I am Ruby Gilbert."

"Forgive my terrible manners, Miss Gilbert. My shop is little used and I tend to get rather lost in my other work." Mr Phoenix frowns down at his scorched sleeve. "If you will take a seat in my study, I will see what I can do for you."

Mr. Phoenix lifts aside the velvet curtain and Ruby steps under the arch on the far side. Worn stone steps lead down to into a jeweller's workshop with a forge, workbenches and racks of tools. Gold and silver glint in the lamplight and the air is heavy with smoke. At the far end of the workshop a door opens onto a book lined study with a Persian carpet and a pair of comfortable armchairs. A lamp stands on a table by one of the chairs and a fire burns in the hearth.

The sparrow flits over Ruby's shoulder and perches on the mantlepiece below a picture in an ornate wooden frame. The picture shows a woman with long dark hair and halo of seven stars, walking across the surface of an ocean. In the background are four hills, each one topped by castle. In the top left corner of the picture, standing on a cloud, is a winged figure bearing a human skull in one hand and a rose in the other. In the foreground stand an armoured knight, with a head like the sun, and a woman with a head like a crescent moon. The longer Ruby looks at the picture the more detail she sees; the wings sprouting from the knights feet and the snake curling in the grass, the fish leaping from the water and the owl on the moon woman's shoulder.

"That picture is called the Rosarium," says Mr. Phoenix. "Many secrets are hidden there."

"Who is the woman with the crown of stars?" asks Ruby.

Solomon Phoenix fixes her with a penetrating look. "There is clearly far more to you than meets the eye," he says. "Perhaps, if you would take a seat, we can begin to unravel the reason for your visit."

They sit opposite each other in front of the fire. The sparrow sits on the mantlepiece, its dark eyes glittering in the lamplight.

"The bottles of water on the counter may have made you think of me as a charlatan," says Solomon Phoenix." But I do possess a measure of True Sight." He takes a bundle of blue silk from a shelf by the fire and unfolds the cloth to reveal a smooth ball of milk-white crystal the size of a man's fist. When he sets the ball upon the table the lamplight catches in its depths, making swirling knots of stars.

The old man passes his hand over the crystal and peers into it.

"You are searching for something," he says, his eyes rising for a moment to meet Ruby's. "We are all searching for something, of course; I do not need the stone to tell me that. " Solomon Phoenix looks deeper into the glimmering crystal. "I see you standing on a gallows platform and a tall rider approaching on a black horse. I see a ship tossed on the sea. I see a young man kneeling before a terrible queen and a diamond falling into a fathomless lake. I see a silver salmon swimming through a veil of stars and I see a burning book. I see you running in the mist, surrounded by shadows." Mr Phoenix frowns and wipes the crystal with the sleeve of his gown. "Most strange." He looks up at Ruby. "The things that the stone shows are like pictures seen in a dream. Their significance is often hard to fathom."

"Did you truly see those things?" asks Ruby.

"I did," says Mr. Phoenix. "Did they mean something to you?"

Despite his unusual manner, Ruby's instincts tell her that she can trust Solomon Phoenix.

The old man listens in silence as Ruby tells him the tale of her flight from Squire Colby and the ride with Davey into Faerie, of her return to the Waking World and of her quest to find the lost diamond.

"The curse placed upon the Diamond may explain the mist in the crystal," says Mr Phoenix. "The Showing Stone will help us no more. But I have an idea where to look next."

The old man goes to the book case, takes down a leather bound volume and sets it on the table. The title page is written in ink the colour of dried blood:
Lapidus mysterium - a work by the hand of Johannes Orpheus.

"If there is any record of the Diamond then it will be in here," says Solomon Phoenix. "I have only recently acquired this book, after its author was sadly vaporised in an unfortunate furnace accident." The old man sighs. " Alchemy has its perils, I am afraid." He begins to leaf through the pages. "Johannes Orpheus was quite systematic in his work. Agate, Arsenic, Bloodstone, Carbuncle, Diamond ..."

Mr Phoenix leans close over the book, his brows furrowed in concentration. "Here!" He smiles up at Ruby, his blue eyes bright.

"The History of the diamond known as the Fairy Star.
This fabled gem was stolen from the crown of the Queen of Faerie and carried to the waking world by Loki the trickster. It contains a great deal of Queen Mab's own magic and the possession of it is said to give the owner the power to bind Queen Mab to their will. A deadly curse lies upon the gem, causing the death of any mortal who owns it.

There are countless legends surrounding the Faerie Star, but the first reliable record places it in the possession of a Russian nobleman by the name of Alexander Kursk, who acquired it in a game of dice with a mysterious traveller in the year 1697. Alexander Kursk lost his life in duel the very next day and the gem passed into the hands of the doctor who attended to him. The doctor took the jewel and gave it as a gift to the Duke of Milan, in return for the Duke's daughter's hand in marriage. On the wedding night the Duke's castle was destroyed by a fire. The only survivor was a young servant, who carried the gem away with him to Genoa, where he took a ship bound for Tangiers. The ship was waylaid by pirates and the gem stolen by the pirate, Carlos O'Scura, also known as The Terror of Tortuga. He wore the diamond on a gold chain about his neck, believing that it brought him good luck, but he was decapitated by a canon-ball in an engagement with an English ship off the coast of Martinique. The diamond was taken from the pirate by the English captain but its current whereabouts are unknown."

"Here the account ends," says Solomon Phoenix. The old man halts for a moment, lost in thought.
"Three days ago I received a visit from a jeweller who wanted my advice about setting a large diamond. The gem was too valuable to be taken out of his workshop and I had to accompany Mr. Lucien to his shop, where he swore me to secrecy. The diamond was astonishing; the most perfect that I have ever seen. It was as large as you describe and as clear as water. It had an unearthly light to it; I can quite believe that it was enchanted."
"Can you take me to the workshop?" says Ruby.
A shadow crosses Solomon Phoenix's face.
"It seems that the tale of the curse upon the Faerie Star may be true, for Mr Lucien was killed yesterday night, stuck down by robbers in his shop."
"And the diamond?"
"The thieves took everything," says Mr Phoenix. "If the diamond had not already been returned to its owner then the robbers have it now."
"Who owned the diamond?"
"Lord Winter," says Mr Phoenix. "He wanted it set into a necklace for his wife."
Ruby remembers the carpet laid out over the cobbles of Bond Street. She remembers the white faced lady

in the blue dress and the surly doorman who barred her way. She had been so near to it!

"Where does Lord Winter live?" Asks Ruby.

"Lord Winter is the chief of the admiralty. Before that he had a long career in the British Navy. It is possible that he captained a war ship in his youth."

"And took the diamond from that pirate?"

"Perhaps," nods Mr Phoenix. "It would have been some years ago. Lord Winter seems to have survived the curse. But if the diamond were kept in a vault in the intervening years then its malign power might have been lessened."

Ruby is on her feet, unable to contain her excitement. If Lady Winter called at Maison Lucien yesterday then it must have been to collect the Faerie Star.

"I shall try to discover the fate of the Diamond," says Mr Phoenix. "Let me know where I might send word."

"To Hawkins Yard in Hackney," says Ruby. On sudden impulse, she reaches into her cloak and takes out the golden leaf. "Please, take this as payment for your help."

"Faerie gold?" Solomon Phoenix lifts the leaf so that the light shines through it. "It seems to have a life of its own, more like a plant than a mineral." He looks at Ruby. "This is priceless - I cannot keep it."

"Then look after it for me," says Ruby. "It's so delicate that I'm afraid I'll break it."

Mr Phoenix nods his head.

"I shall look after it very well," he says.

Chapter 9 - Wildflowers in Midwinter

"Where did you get this?" asks Mr Famish, holding up the silver sixpence.

"I found it," says Jimmy.

Mr Famish leans closer, putting his nose to Jimmy's cheek.

"I can smell a lie," he whispers. "I can sniff 'em out like a terrier scenting a rat." He grabs Jimmy's ear and twists it until Jimmy squeals. "Where did you get it?"

"Ruby Gilbert -"

"I told you to watch her, not rob her, you ignorant scum."

Mr Famish deals Jimmy a vicious blow and drops the sixpence in his own pocket.

"You know the rules. All takings are mine."

The cellar is lit by a candle set in a cracked saucer. In the far corner Rosie Twigg covers her face with her hands.

"Just do as he says, Jimmy," Rosie whispers to herself. *"Don't give him any reason to hurt you."*

"Let's see what else you've got," says Mr Famish. He pins Jimmy against the wall with one hand and rummages in his pockets with the other. He pulls out the battered remains of the eel pie, throws it on the floor and grinds it under his boot heel. He reaches into Jimmy's other pocket and pulls out the posy of wildflowers.

Rosie Twigg gives a gasp of wonder when she see the cornflowers and poppies, glowing like jewels in the candle light. Jimmy makes a grab for the posy.

"That's for Rosie."

Mr Famish cuffs Jimmy round the head and he cowers back.

"Flowers - in the dead of winter - they must have cost a fortune. Where did you get 'em?"

Jimmy doesn't know what to say. Mr Famish won't believe him if he tells the truth and he's bound to know if Jimmy tries to lie. When Jimmy makes no reply Mr Famish grabs his arm and twists it up behind his back.

"Where are they from?"

"Ruby Gilbert made 'em grow," says Jimmy. "She made 'em grow in the hay. She's an enchantress."

Mr Famish slams Jimmy back against the wall.

"One more lie and you are dog meat," Mr Famish hisses. He tosses the flowers away into the darkness. "Tell me about Ruby Gilbert. Where has she been?"

Mr Famish might be able to smell a lie but he can't see into Jimmy's mind. Jimmy wants to stay true to Ruby but he fears Mr Famish's whip more than anything.

  Best to stay as near the truth as he can.

"I heard her say she was off to see a fortune teller in Covent Garden," says Jimmy. "She's desperate to find the diamond."

"I never mentioned a diamond," whispers Mr Famish. "How do you know about it?"

Jimmy's mind is racing. Mr Famish is in a wild mood and there's no telling what he might do.

"I heard her talking to one of the jewellers," says Jimmy quickly. "She's been all over town looking for a diamond but no-one knows anything about it."

"Why didn't you follow her to Covent Garden?"

"I came here to tell you, like you said. I thought -"

"Shut up."

Mr Famish lets go of Jimmy and he slides down the wall to sit cowering at the man's feet.

"Get after Ruby Gilbert again," says Mr Famish. "Don't let her see you and don't come back until you've something useful for me." He bares his teeth at Jimmy. "No more lies, boy!"

Jimmy lowers his eyes and nods.

Mr Famish turns to Rosie, sitting silent and wide eyed on the edge of the circle of candle light.

"Get your good dress on," he says. "I've work for you later. There's a house in Chelsea that's ripe for the taking."

When Mr Famish is gone Rosie creeps over to the corner where the flowers were flung. She brings them back to the candle and straightens the stems up as best she can.

She looks up at Jimmy.

"Did she really do magic?"

"I seen her do it," says Jimmy.

"Wildflowers in midwinter!" says Rosie, her face bright with joy.

Chapter 10 - Dark Blue Silk

  The letter from Mr Phoenix arrives the next evening.
Ruby is sitting at the kitchen table with Tom and
Charlie Angel, who has just charmed Hannah into
giving him a second helping of treacle tart.
"Is that from another one of your admirers?" asks
Charlie.
Ruby ignores him, breaks open the wax seal on the
envelope and begins to read.

My Dear Miss Gilbert
I trust that this finds you well. I have enquired as to
the whereabouts of the item that we discussed and
can confirm that it was returned to its owner before
the unfortunate events of two nights ago. The house
that you seek is on the river, near Kew.
Please take greatest care in your search. It is a
perilous undertaking.
If there is anything else that I can do to assist you
then do not hesitate to let me know.
Yours sincerely
Solomon Phoenix

Ruby looks up at Charlie and Tom.
"Do you know where Lord Winter lives?" she asks.
"It's a grand house," says Charlie."Down Richmond
way,"
"Is the diamond there?" asks Tom.
Ruby pauses before she answers. She is still not
certain of Charlie.
"I need to find out," says Ruby. "Will you help me?"

"I'm your man," says Charlie. "I know all about getting into places."

The next afternoon they meet up in the hay loft. Ruby has searched the place thoroughly for Jimmy Twigg but found no sign of him. She asked Hannah and Sid about taking Jimmy on as a stable boy. They agreed to it, but Ruby has not seen Jimmy since she gave him the sixpence.

"I had a good look at the place," says Charlie Angel, picking straw from the sleeve of his coat. "The gossip in the kitchen is that Lady Winter has a new necklace with a diamond in it as big as an apple."

"What else?" asks Ruby.

"The house is well guarded. Lord Winter has a small army of his own men, all armed to the teeth. It would be a hard place to rob." He grins. "If it weren't for one thing ..."

"Yes?"

"Lady Winter is holding a masked ball on Saturday night. All you need is an invitation." With a theatrical flourish Charlie takes a card from his pocket and lays it on the hay beside Ruby. The thick white vellum is printed in gold and black ink.

Lord and Lady Winter invite you to a Carnival of Lights and Masked Ball at Winter Hall on the evening of the 8th of February
The festivities begin at Seven O'clock.

"I managed to convince the housemaid to steal this for me," says Charlie

"What did you promise her in return?" asks Tom.

"I might have mentioned something about marriage," says Charlie airily. He produces a letter from another pocket and hands it to Tom "You're a talented fellow. I bet you could make a copy of Lady Winter's signature and put Ruby's name at the top of the card."

Tom studies the letter.

"It's from Lady Winter to her sister in Bristol," says Charlie with a shrug. "It got lost on the way to the mail coach."

"You're not expecting me to go?" says Ruby. "They'll know me at once for an imposter."

"It's a masked ball," says Charlie. "Everyone's face will be covered. All you need is a nice dress. We can spruce up one of your uncle's carriages and me and Tom can be your footmen."

Ruby stares at Charlie Angel in disbelief. Ruby had imagined that Jack Shadow would be the one to take to diamond, sneaking into Winter Hall in the dead of night and escaping on a fast horse. Charlie Angel's crazy plan might get her into the Hall but the idea of disguising herself as a member of the nobility terrifies Ruby far more than the idea of returning to the life of a highwayman.

"They say that Lady Winter will be wearing the diamond at the ball," says Charlie. "There's bound to be a way to nab it." He smiles his most winning smile. "What do you reckon?"

Ruby knows where the diamond is and she would be a fool not to risk going after it. She might not get another chance like this.

"I'll need a dress," she says.

Jimmy Twigg slips the loose tile back into place and slides silently down the slope of the hayloft roof. He creeps along the top of the wall and scrambles down the ivy onto the road. This is something that Mr Famish will want to know about.

Ruby leaves Tom and Charlie with the cart while she goes into Mrs Probert's dress shop. Tom and Charlie already have their black and gold footman's livery, "borrowed" from a friend of Charlie's who works at the Laundry on Wormwood Street.

Miss Probert is a narrow, hatchet faced woman with eyes like needles.

"Dresses are two Shillings a day and you'll leave me a Guinea as security," she says, looking at Ruby's travel worn clothes with distaste.

"I haven't seen the dresses yet," begins Ruby.

"And you won't see them until you pay me," says Miss Probert. "I'll not have you putting your grubby fingers on my fine silks before I see your money."

Ruby's fingers are quite clean but there is no use in arguing. She hands Miss Probert Two Shillings and a Guinea and is led into the back room where the dresses are kept.

The back room of the shop stinks of stale perfume and mothballs. The dresses are mostly fluffy confections in silk and lace. None of them are anything like new and most of them have been mended several times.

Ruby chooses a simple dark blue dress with a matching pair of shoes. It looks better than most of the others and she guesses that she could ride a horse in it if she had to. She refuses the whalebone corset offered by Miss Probert.

From the selection of masks, Ruby chooses a simple black velvet eye mask decorated with silver stars. The outfit is slipped into a box and tied up with a ribbon.

"Now that you're all togged up," says Tom, as they ride away. "You'll need to find yourself a name. I don't think plain old Ruby Gilbert will look right on the invitation card."
Ruby grins:
"I shall be Lady Charlotte Vesper."

Chapter 11 - Shadow Fire

They fill the silent hall. Tall and pale, their faces thin and cruel, their eyes dark. Their high shoulders are strangely hunched and their armour is scorched black. There are swords and axes in their hands and around their necks are heavy rings of iron.

"I have heard a whisper from the Waking World," says Lord Ruin. "A mortal sorcerer seeks to make a pact with us"

"How could any mortal aid us?" snarls Torment. "Can they remove our shackles?" she puts up a hand to her iron neck ring and shudders at its biting touch.

"He offers us a path into the Waking World," replies Lord Ruin.

"Shall we be freed from this place?" asks Torment. "Shall we walk in solid form upon the earth?"

Lord Ruin shakes his head.

"The hour is not come for that - not yet. We shall go by night in shadow shape and make a reaping such as has not been seen in many ages of men. We shall feed and we shall grow strong again."

"Why go into the world as ghosts, only to be cast back when the gate closes? We have endured a life of shadows long enough."

"Be silent!" hisses Lord Ruin. "I am Lord of the Wytch Fire. Heed me or be cast into the flames!"

Torment lowers her head, her proud eyes full of hatred.

The ash pit before Lord Ruin's throne is piled deep with bones and the flames are cold and pale, filled with silent, screaming faces.

"The spirits of the dead have spoken to me," says Lord Ruin. "They tell of a time to come when Queen Mab's power will be broken. And when she falls, the curse that binds us will be no more. Our shackles will be broken and we shall unleash our hunger upon the Nine Worlds!"

Chapter 12 - The Winter Ball

The carriage turns a corner and Winter Hall appears through the trees, glittering like a faerie palace. Every one of the windows is lit up and the grounds are hung with lanterns. Snowflakes of mirrored glass are strung in the trees along the avenue and the sound of flutes and violins comes drifting through the night.

It is strange to be riding alone in the back of the carriage while Tom and Charlie sit up at the front. Ruby huddles down into her borrowed coat, thrown over her shoulders at the last minute by Sid, as they left Hawkins Yard. She should have a fur wrap if she is to take the part of a Society Lady arriving at a winter ball, but it was too late for that. Besides, Ruby likes Sid's old stable coat better than any fur. It is warmer and it smells comfortingly of horses.

The carriage draws up on the gravel outside the house and a servant dressed in blue livery and a silver mask comes forward to open the door. Ruby throws the coat off and pushes it out of sight. She shivers at the sudden cold, takes a deep breath and steps down. A blue carpet has been laid out over the gravel and a line of servants in silver masks bow low as she passes. Heart thumping, Ruby tries to remember everything that she practiced last night in the kitchen.

"Keep your back as straight as a poker and take tiny steps," said Hannah. "Put your nose in the air, as if you've just smelled something nasty."

Ruby's first attempts to Walk Like A Lady had Hannah and Katy in hysterics. Seth sat by the fire, smoking his pipe and smiling. He couldn't see Ruby's ridiculous parade but the laughter was infectious. "If you want to convince them that you are nobility," he said."You must walk as if the whole world belongs to you."

  Ruby remembers the way that Queen Mab commanded obedience from her servants, how she made the sea rise up and summoned the wind to carry Ruby back through the gates of the Waking World. She closes her eyes and imagines herself as powerful and terrible as the Faerie Queen.

  The ball is nothing but a carnival and if Ruby plays her part then no-one will suspect who she really is. It is no different to being Jack Shadow. She wishes for a pistol in her belt but she suspects that would rather spoil the effect.

  Charlie Angel jumps down from the front seat of the carriage to follow Ruby. He wears his borrowed livery and a golden cherub mask. Ruby would rather have Tom with her but Charlie has even less skill with horses and the carriage must be ready in case they have to make a quick escape.

  A silver masked footman bows and holds out a silver platter. Ruby stares at it blankly. Something is clearly expected of her - but what? Her sense of relief at having managed to walk from the carriage to the house without anyone spotting her as an imposter dissolves.

Charlie steps forward and places the invitation card on the platter.

"My mistress, Lady Charlotte Vesper," he says to the servant. "Lately arrived from Genoa."

The servant lifts the tray and turns away. Charlie nudges Ruby forward and they follow.

The entrance hall is huge enough the hold the cottage she grew up in, with room to spare for the barn. The floor is made from squares of polished black and white marble and an enormous crystal chandelier hangs from the vaulted ceiling. A wide marble staircase curves up to the upper floors and the walls are hung with pictures in gold frames. Guests mill about and servants stand in readiness along the walls. Dressed alike in light blue silk livery and silver masks, the servants look like mechanical toys waiting to be wound.

The footman leads them through the echoing hall toward the ballroom. Inside is a riot of colour and laughter. Ladies in wide skirted dresses, glittering jewels and powdered wigs piled high upon their heads, gentlemen in evening suits and dress uniforms of red and blue and gold. And the masks; eagles, lions, dragons and stags, horned devils, unicorns and all manner of fantasies in sequins, silver and feathers.

A huge man in a blue coat and a silver mask leans down and takes the card from the footman's tray. The footman whispers into the majordomo's ear. He lifts the card with a flourish and calls out in a booming voice:

"Lady Charlotte Vesper of Genoa!"

Ruby steps forward and curtsies. A sea of masked faces turn to her. Some of the gentlemen bow, a couple of ladies smile and return her curtsey, while the others turn away to gossip behind their fans. Ruby keeps her back straight and her expression confident as she strides into the room. She can guess what is being said behind her back; she is an unknown girl in a second hand dress. How long before she is found out?

Ruby does not care what these people think of her, just as long as she can find the Faerie Star and rescue Davey.

A masked servant sweeps up with a tray of champagne. Ruby takes a glass and moves on through he crowd, walking as if she knows exactly where she is going. Her plan is to find a seat in a quiet corner and wait for Lady Winter to appear.

The few chairs in the ballroom are already taken by gossiping groups of ladies but Ruby finds a quiet place to stand next to a tall ice statue of a swan. She looks out over the gathering, at the painted masks and dresses hung with pearls, at the servants moving through the crowd with trays of champagne. Charlie taps her arm and points to the silent, silver masked men standing against the walls. They are dressed in darker blue uniforms and have swords and pistols at their sides.

"Those are Lord Winter's hired men," whispers Charlie. "A bunch of cut throats by all accounts. They've been with him since his Navy days."

"Where is Genoa?" asks Ruby.

"It's in Italy," says Charlie. "I thought it best to tell 'em you were from some far-off place. That way, if you make a mistake they can put it down to you being a foreigner."

"That's fine until they try talking to me in Italian."

"Lord and Lady Winter!" Calls the majordomo.

A hush descends and the guests all turn to the door.

Lord Winter is a tall man dressed in a dark blue naval uniform and a golden mask depicting a bearded sea god. Lady Winter is dressed in pale blue silk and wears a silvery mask studded with pearls and shells. Around her neck is the Faerie Star. There is a collective indrawn breath as the crowd catch sight of the diamond. Clear and brilliant, it sparkles with an unearthly light, sending rainbows dancing over the floor at Lady Winter's feet.

Ruby remembers the sight of Queen Mab's crown and for an instant she is transported back to the twilight glade. The candles above her become the flickering stars of Faerie and the guests become Mab's courtiers, dressed in fur and silver.

Behind Lord and Lady Winter stand two armed men in dark blue uniforms. As the hosts step out into the crowd the masked men keep pace, never straying more than a couple of steps behind.

"They aren't taking any chances," whispers Charlie. "We'll have to look sharp if we're to get the diamond."

Ruby cannot take her eyes from the Faerie Star. To be so near to her goal and unable to reach it is almost unbearable.

"The chamber maid told me that Lady Winter won't do more than a couple of dances," says Charlie. "You keep an eye on her and follow close when she leaves. Outside the ballroom is our best chance. I'll do what I can to create a distraction so you can nab the Diamond."

"That's not much of plan," says Ruby, lifting the champagne to her lips.

"You got a better idea?" shrugs Charlie.

A gong sounds and the majordomo calls out again.

"Ladies and gentlemen. Pray attention for the first dance of the evening."

There is a flurry of movement as people move back to clear the floor. Lord and Lady Winter step to the centre and the music begins. Everyone watches as they move gracefully across the dance floor, the Faerie Star glittering in the candle light.

"It looks so beautiful," whispers Ruby."It is hard to believe that it is cursed."

 The first dance ends and the guests begin to partner up and join their hosts on the dance floor. Ruby keeps her head down and tries to keep out of sight behind the ice sculpture but a red coated soldier in a peacock mask appears and bows before her.

"Captain Prim, at your service, madam. May I have the honour of his dance?"

Ruby had not planned on dancing. She has taken many a turn about the market square in Bascome but never practiced this kind of stiff legged parade.

  Charlie nudges her in the back.

"Go on!" he hisses. "It'll look wrong if you refuse."

Ruby curtsies to the man, takes his hand, and he leads her out into the crowd. She is alone and swimming in deep water.

The music begins, the soldier bows, puts a hand on Ruby's shoulder, lifts her hand and begins to step in time. Ruby does her best to follow, glancing desperately at the other dancers to get some clue as to what she should be doing.

"I have not seen you at Winter Hall before, Lady Vesper," says the soldier.

Ruby has no idea what an Italian accent might sound like but she remembers the old French lace seller from Truro market and does her best to mimic her.

"I am newly arrived from Italy," says Ruby.

"I have been to Venice, of course," says the soldier."The most beautiful city on earth."

"Of course," mumbles Ruby.

"Did you attend many balls in Italy?" asks the peacock soldier.

"No," says Ruby. "I am afraid that my family is not rich."

The soldier's manner becomes cooler at once:

"London in winter must be a great shock after the Mediterranean sun."

Ruby steps hard onto the soldiers toes and hears him gasp with pain.

"Simply awful," says Ruby.

She treads on the soldier's feet several times more and when the music stops he bows quickly and limps away as fast as he can.

Ruby is attempting to escape from the dance floor when a tall gentleman in a dark suit and a fox mask bows and puts his hand out. Ruby shrugs. The man takes Ruby's hand and the music begins again. Fox Face has clearly already helped himself to his share of the champagne and is quite unsteady on his feet. Ruby does her best to stop him from colliding with the other dancers and says as little as possible. The man seems not to notice. He talks incessantly and seems to require no reply from Ruby, leaving her free to keep her eyes on Lady Winter and steer her drunken partner closer.

By the time the dance has finished Ruby is only a few feet away from Lady Winter. She is hoping that Fox Face will ask her for another dance, as he is so easy to control, but he bows and hurries away, intent on drinking Lord Winter's cellar dry.

A tall figure steps from the crowd and Ruby looks up into a pair of glittering eyes framed in a jet black wolf mask.

"Lady Vesper," says the wolf faced gentleman. "May I have the next dance?"

Without waiting for reply the wolf faced man takes Ruby's hand. He puts his other hand on her shoulder, grasps it hard and leans close.

"You have taken a new name, Ruby Gilbert, but you cannot hide from me."

Terror takes her - so sudden and cold that she gasps. She knows that voice; it is Josia Colby. He is the reason that she and her family fled Cornwall. He killed her mother, he blinded her father and he would have killed Ruby too, If Davey had not bargained away his life to Queen Mab in order to save her.

How could Josia Colby have recognised her? Ruby put on her mask as soon as they left Hackney.

The music begins again and there is no more time to think.

Chapter 13 - Behind the Mask

 "I wonder what would our hosts would do if I told them who you really are?" says Josia Colby, leaning his wolf head down so that the dark muzzle brushes Ruby's cheek.

  She forces herself to breathe. Her heart screams at her to run but she knows that she must wait; she has to find out why Josia Colby is here.

"What would they do if I told them that you are a sorcerer who drinks human blood?" she hisses.

"I no longer require the Elixir. My power has grown since we last met."

"You are still a monster."

"This is my world. It does not matter what you say. Who will Lord Winter believe? His trusted business associate or a dung shoveler's daughter dressed as a duchess?"

"Why would Lord Winter trust you?"

"Lord Winter's plantations in the America's rely on my ships to transport the sugar and the slaves. He will not want to upset me."

Ruby looks at the ballroom with new eyes. The fine house is built upon slavery and the wealth of its master is built upon suffering. She has seen slave ships at the docks at Plymouth and she has heard how the captured souls are treated.

"I have more earthly power than you could understand," says Squire Colby. "And you are quite alone here. Your only hope is do exactly as I tell you."
Josia Colby is a slaver. Is there no end to his evil? Ruby fights back the urge to be sick as fear and disgust overwhelm her.
"You are not my master," she says.
"Soon I will be master of everything. You had a chance to take my life but you lacked the strength to do it. I have renewed myself ten-fold since then. I have Queen Mab's book of magic and before the night is through I shall have the Faerie Star. The Nine Worlds will bow down before me and the legions of darkness will be mine to command. There will be no-one to stand in my way."

For a moment, Ruby's courage fails her. She outwitted Squire Colby once before but she had help; she had Davey and the magic that cost him so dearly. Who does she have now? She looks desperately through the crowd for Charlie Angel but there is no sign of him.
"You are alone."
Squire Colby's words begin to weave their hypnotic spell. Ruby feels herself slipping into a trance, the music carrying her as the web of enchantment tightens around her.

When the music stops, Squire Colby takes a step back and bows. He still has tight hold of Ruby's hand but her mind clears a little. She sees Lady Winter take the arm of a woman in a green dress. The two women turn and walk away, toward the door of the ballroom, the Faerie Star glittering on Lady Winter's chest.

The sight of the diamond snaps Ruby back to her senses.

She might be alone but she is not powerless.

She pulls back from the Squire. She slaps her hand against the cheek of his mask and screams at the top of her voice:

"Take your hands off me. You are no gentleman!"

A shocked hush falls as the dancers turn to stare at the tall man in the wolf mask looming over the terrified girl.

A red coated soldier in a lion mask puts his hand to the hilt of his sword and steps forward:

"Unhand the Lady at once."

The Squire snarls with fury but he lets go of Ruby's hand.

"This young woman is not what she seems."

"He is a brute!" says Ruby, grasping the soldier's arm. "He said the most awful things to me." She puts her hands to her face and breaks into a fit of very realistic sobbing. She turns for the door and the crowd part for her.

"You will apologise," says the soldier.

"I shall do no such thing," replies Squire Colby.

The Squire steps after Ruby but two more men block his path. He glares at them through the slitted eye sockets of his wolf mask but he makes no further move to follow.

"She is an imposter," he says. "A jewel thief, come to steal Lady Winter's diamond. All of this is a ploy, nothing more."

Everyone stares at Squire Colby, many in disgust, but those nearby are already falling under the spell of his voice. Ruby knows that it will not be long before he has charmed them all. She has only a moment to reach the door of the ballroom.

Two others move through the crowd; a small man in a rat mask and large man wearing a porcelain clown's face. They have been watching the dance from a shadowed corner, and now they begin to elbow their way through the dancers toward Ruby.

Aside from the silver masked servants standing to attention against the walls, the only people in the vast entrance hall are Lady Winter, her two guards and the woman in the green dress.

Where is Charlie Angel? He should be here by now.

Ruby recognises the lady in green as the servant girl who made the doorman at Maison Lucien grovel for fallen coins.

The maid curtsies and walks away, leaving Lady Winter alone, with the blue coated guards standing at a respectful distance.

The front door of Winter Hall is only a short sprint away. Ruby could be out and away to her carriage in a moment; she could be safe from Squire Colby. But the diamond is here, right before her eyes, glittering against the silk of Lady Winter's dress.

Even as she steps forward, Ruby hears it; a distant creaking, barely audible over the music from the ballroom. A fine scatter of snow drifts down onto the polished marble floor.

Snow?

Ruby looks up.

The ceiling stretches above her like a vast white flower, curling petals unfurling about a central rose, where the chandelier hangs on its iron chains. But there is a crack running through the heart of the rose, spilling plaster dust into the hall. The crack widens with a sudden snap and the chandelier trembles.

Ruby is running before she has time to think about it. Lady Winter turns toward the sound of Ruby's running feet. She sees the plaster dust hanging in the air between them and lifts her head.

The chandelier is as big as small house, supported by four sturdy iron chains, but the ceiling around the chain fixings is sagging and crazed with cracks.

Ruby runs faster.

The chandelier lurches to one side and the light in the hall dims as the candles tip in their crystal dishes. Lady Winter gasps and puts her hand up to shield herself from the rain of molten wax.

Every atom of Ruby's being is concentrated on running. She hears her dress rip but she pays no attention.

Lady Winter stands paralysed with shock, staring dumbly upwards as the chandelier breaks free of its moorings. Stately as a galleon, turning in the wind, the chandelier plunges away from the ceiling. A silver masked footman screams and a hundred candles gutter out at the same time.

Ruby takes another leaping stride. She cannons into Lady Winter and the great blossom of Lady Winter's blue silk dress crumples. Beneath the silk and petticoats Lady Winter is a slight figure and Ruby easily manages to lift her off her feet. The wig falls from Lady Winter's head and the shell covered mask slips to the floor and shatters. The chain holding the Faerie star snaps and the diamond falls, flashing with white fire.

Ruby carries Lady Winter onward in a desperate, half-stumbling run. She manages three more steps before she loses her balance and they fall together, skidding away over the polished floor towards the wall.

The chandelier lands with a cataclysmic crash, shattering the marble tiles and shaking the house to its foundations.

From his perch on the window ledge Jimmy Twig has a ringside view of the fall of the chandelier. He sees Ruby Gilbert and the old lady in the blue dress escape by a whisker and go skidding into the wall. One of Lady Winter's guards manages to jump clear but the other is hit by a falling timber and is laid out headlong on the floor.

The sounds of destruction fade and a shaft of light from the ballroom stabs out over the snowfall of shattered glass.

A woman in the ballroom screams and a second later her voice is joined by a hundred others, men and women alike, shrieking as if the world has ended.

Jimmy is quite safe, hidden behind a curtain, twenty feet up on a ledge overlooking the entrance hall. On the floor directly below him something glitters in the half light.

Jimmy is not the only one to have spotted the Faerie Star. One of the masked servants is running forward and two more men are running from the ballroom; a small man in a rat mask and a giant with a clown's face.

The footman reaches the jewel first and grabs it up. That must be one of Famish's men; he said they'd be dressed as footman, one in light blue, the other in black and gold. The falling chandelier wasn't part of the plan but it's a piece of luck for the thieves.

Jimmy catches his breath; he shouldn't be here! He is supposed to be outside by now, ready to take the jewel from the footman as he runs out of the front door. There is a carriage waiting at the far side of Lord Winter's estate and inside that carriage is Mr Famish.

Jimmy cringes back, already feeling the bite of Mr Famish's whip. He turns to the window but before he can open it, a pistol shot rings out.

There is a flash of orange light and the silver masked footman falls back, gripping his shoulder. The mask slips and Jimmy sees the face of Sniffer Cole, one of Famish's burglars. The diamond falls from Sniffer's hand and the blue coated guard steps forward. The guard lunges for the diamond but the rat masked man gets there first.

"That is Lord Winter's property," shouts the guard. His pistol empty so he draws his sword. Clown Face draws a sword of his own and Rat Mask takes out a dagger.

"Finders keepers," says Rat Mask, darting his hand down to grab the diamond.

Clown Face steps to block the guard's way and Rat Mask turns to run but he has hardly taken a step when a second pistol fires. The bullet hits Rat Mask on the hand and he drops the jewel with a shriek of pain.

Ruby Gilbert steps out of the shadows. She has two pistols, taken from the fallen guard. She tosses the empty one aside and points the loaded one at Rat Mask.

"Stop right there, Mr Furey," she says. She jerks the pistol sideways to point at the clown faced giant. "You too, Ransome."

The masked men halt.

"Ruby Gilbert," hisses Mr Furey. "We should have killed you a long time ago." He cradles his injured hand to his chest and takes a firm grip on his dagger. "We'll finish the job properly this time."

Mr Furey takes a step forward but he thinks better of it when Ruby flicks the pistol barrel back to point at his heart. Keeping her eyes on the two men, Ruby kneels down to pick up the diamond.

Shafts of yellow light cut through the gloom as a group of men come running from the ballroom carrying lanterns.

"Thieves, My Lord!" calls the guard. "They're after the diamond."

Rat face and Clown turn and run. Sniffer Cole tries to follow but he is brought down by the guard's outstretched leg.

"Time to get out of here," thinks Jimmy Twigg.

Ruby has a clear path to the front door. She has the diamond in one hand and a loaded pistol in the other.

There is a crackle of boots on broken glass and she turns to see a masked figure step through the swirling haze of plaster dust. He is tall and broad and wears the face of Neptune, God of the sea.

"Perhaps I should take the diamond," says Lord Winter, putting out his hand. "Before anyone else tries to steal it?"

Behind Lord Winter are three of his men, all armed with swords and pistols.

Ruby has no choice. With a sinking heart, she hands the diamond to Lord Winter. He nods his head in thanks and puts the Faerie Star into the pocket of his jacket. He takes off his mask and Ruby sees a man of about sixty, with thick grey hair and side whiskers. He has a scar on his left cheek and grey, unforgiving eyes.

"For a moment it almost looked as if you were thinking of taking the jewel for yourself?" he says coldly.

"Robert! She saved my life," says Lady Winter, coming to her husband's side, her eyes wild with shock. "If it hadn't been for this brave girl I would have been crushed to death."

Lord Winter raises an eyebrow and looks over at the guard who has Sniffer Cole in an armlock.

"It's quite true, My Lord" say the man." The young lady saved your wife from the falling chandelier and then took the diamond back off the thieves." The guard winks at Ruby." That was a good shot, Miss."

Lord Winter turns to nod at his men and they turn to run after Ransome and Furey.

"I am greatly indebted to you," says Lord Winter. "You are clearly a remarkable young woman. May I ask your name?"

"Lady Charlotte Vesper."

"Oh my!" shrieks Lady Winter, taking hold of Ruby's arm and pointing down at the fallen guard. "Is that poor man dead?"

The plaster dust has begun to settle, covering everything in a haze of white. The fallen man's face is ghostly pale, stained vivid scarlet with blood from his injured head.

Lord Winter kneels beside the fallen man, grabs the front of his jacket and slaps him across the face. The man groans and gives a cough.

"An English sailor's skull is pretty thick," says Lord Winter, dropping the man back to the floor."I think he'll live."

Lady Winter looks around at the devastation.

"What has happened to our home, Robert?"

Lord Winter scowls:

"Lady Vesper," he says. "Might I ask you to accompany my wife to her room. She is clearly in a state of shock. One of my men will go with you."

Ruby wants to flee Winter Hall but to run now would only arouse suspicion. She nods, takes hold of Lady Winter's arm and they follow the man with the lantern up the marble staircase.

Chapter 14 - Silver and Grey

Jimmy slips out of the window and slides down the drainpipe. There are people running in all directions on the gravel drive; servants in silver masks and guests fleeing to their carriages, all of them far too busy to pay attention to a small boy darting into the bushes.

Jimmy is deep in the woods on the far side of the house when he hears voices ahead. Quick as blinking, he scrambles up the nearest tree and hides in a fold of the branches. The voices come nearer and halt directly below his hiding place. He peeks down to see the two masked men from the hall; Rat Face and Clown.

The small man has taken off his mask but the face underneath is still distinctly rat-like; narrow and spiteful, framed in a mess of long greasy hair. The big man has pushed the china clown face up onto to his bald head like a hat. His face is large and pale and pitted with scars.

"I reckon them stories about the diamond being cursed are true," says the big man. "If Ruby Gilbert hadn't pushed Lady Winter out of the way-"

"I'll snuff her out," hisses Rat Face venomously. He is wrapping a rag around his bleeding hand and muttering curses. "I'll kill her and her whole stinking family."

"What you moaning about?" says the big man.

"You've still got all your fingers 'aint you?" He looks

up at the sky and Jimmy is surprised to see fear in his eyes. "You don't know how lucky you are. The moon's coming out in a minute. You know what that means."

"I've got your chain," mutters Mr Furey. "Don't worry."

"Don't forget to pick up my coat," says the big man."I don't want to lose another."

He tears off his coat, unbuckles his sword belt, and sits down on a tree stump to pull off his boots.

"These are new, don't leave 'em behind."

"I'm not carrying your clobber around all night," mutters Mr Furey. "I'm not a flippin' ladies maid."

The moon slides out from behind the clouds, glinting on the frosty branches. Captain Ransome moans and falls to the ground in a faint.

Before Jimmy's eyes, Captain Ransome begins to change.

He twists and thrashes, his skin swelling and rippling, his face stretching as his nose swells into a snout. His teeth push out, huge and jagged, his fingers curl back into lumpish paws and his shirt rips open to reveal a ridged, hairy spine.

The creature shakes off the remains of the torn clothes and a huge wolf stands up in the moonlight; a dirty grey, awful thing with scraggy fur and an evil light in its yellow eyes.

Jimmy is too terrified to breathe, his mind reeling at the horror of what he has seen.

Mr Furey glares at the beast with an expression of weary contempt.

"You always were an ugly bloke, Ransome, but turning into a werewolf does nothing for your looks."

The wolf growls and takes a step forward, its eyes level with Mr Furey's. The wolf is as tall as Mr Furey but he does not seem the slightest bit afraid of it.

"No funny business," he says. "Remember what the Squire said? You'll get a whipping if you go off on another one of your rampages."

Mr Furey takes a sack from his coat and pulls out a length of iron chain attached to a heavy leather collar. "Stay still, you daft brute," he mutters. "Let me get your collar on."

The wolf submits to the collar and Mr Furey gathers up Captain Ransome's boots, sword and coat. He bundles them into the sack but leaves the rest of the torn clothes where they are.

"We need to make ourselves scarce," says Mr Furey. "They'll be looking for us."

Mr Furey slings the sack over his shoulder and pulls on the chain. The wolf stays where it is, lifting its snout to scent the air. It gives a low growl and turns to look up into the tree - right at Jimmy.

Jimmy tries to scramble higher but his trembling hands slip on the ice-slicked branches. The wolf leaps up, its claws raking into the bark, the impact of its massive bulk shaking the trunk. Jimmy loses his grip and falls backwards, screaming.

Jimmy hits the ground hard but he is on his feet at once, dazed and breathless, his legs running on their own, carrying him away through the bushes. He hears a growl behind him and the next moment the awful beast is on top of him, crushing him to the ground, his nostrils filling with the stench of rotten meat. Jimmy tries to wriggle away but there is nowhere to go.

"Easy now," says Mr Furey. "You can eat later. We've got to get out here."

Jimmy feels the weight lift from him and turns to see Mr Furey hauling the wolf back. At the sight of Jimmy's face the wolf lunges again, snapping its teeth inches from his nose.

"Leave it!" hisses Mr Furey, leaning his whole body back in an attempt to hold the wolf back.

 Jimmy scrabbles away over the cold ground and the wolf follows, snarling and drooling, dragging Mr Furey along behind.

"You'll get us killed, you daft mutt! "

Jimmy crashes through brambles, not caring where he is going. Behind him comes the sound of tearing branches, the thud of heavy paws and the clatter of the loose chain. Jimmy throws himself forward, tumbling out of the bushes onto a wide lawn, bright with moonlight. Ahead of him is Winter Hall, its windows ablaze. If he can reach the hall then he might be safe.

"Come back!" shouts Mr Furey.

Jimmy can hear the crackle of the wolf's paws on the frosty grass behind him. Something moves ahead of him and Jimmy's heart jumps sideways; a second wolf is racing over the lawn towards them. This one is silvery grey, it is smaller than the first one but just as terrible. Jimmy swerves aside, his feet skid out from under him and he goes over on his face. He curls up into ball and waits to be torn apart.

There is a drum of paws in the earth beside Jimmy's head and a swish of fur as the silver wolf runs past him. Jimmy opens his eyes just in time to see the silver wolf slam into the grey wolf's legs, knocking the larger beast down.

The silver wolf pounces on its fallen enemy, sinking its teeth into the grey wolf's neck. The grey gives a snarl and throws the silver wolf off, rolling back up onto its paws, its teeth flashing in the moonlight

Jimmy stares in mute wonder as the two creatures face each other; silver and dirt-grey, pacing back and forth over the grass. The silver wolf is seems to be trying to protect Jimmy, keeping its body between him and the grey wolf. Is it the same creature that he saw at the well in Highgate?

The wolves leap at each other, tussle and fall back. The grey wolf might be bigger but the silver wolf is quick and clever. It makes a snapping lunge at the grey, jumps sideways and slashes at the grey wolf's flank with its claws.

Mr Furey appears at the edge of the lawn.
"Come back here - right now - you mutton headed cur!"
He darts forward and makes a grab for the grey wolf's trailing chain. He gets a grip on it but the grey wolf gives a shake of its body that pulls the chain free again, sending Mr Furey tumbling.

The grey wolf's eyes light on Jimmy and it bounds towards him, the chain rattling along behind. The silver wolf leaps forward and knocks the grey down again.

The silver wolf crouches on the grass, growling, its tail swishing like an angry cat. Inside the animal sounds of the silver wolf's growl, Jimmy hears words: "I made you, whelp! Leave the boy alone."

The grey wolf's reply is a snarl and a snap of its teeth. Eyes rolling in fury, it leaps forward. The silver wolf jumps away but the trailing chain whips through the air and clatters into the silver wolf's front legs, knocking it down. The grey wolf pounces and crushes the silver wolf to the ground, opens its horrid jaws wide and bites down on the silver wolf's neck.

There is a sudden gun shot. The bullet goes wide but the noise startles the grey wolf enough for the silver wolf to wriggle free. It rolls to its paws and backs away, limping. Jimmy sees blood glinting in the silver fur of its right foreleg.

A gang of men with lanterns and rifles are running from the house. Jimmy leaps to his feet and sprints wildly towards them. It doesn't matter what they do to him. It can't be worse than being eaten by wolves.

"Get out of the way - idiot!" yells a tall, grey haired man. "Give me a clear shot."

The man goes down on one knee and raises his rifle. The rest of the men follow suit.

"Not the silver wolf!" shouts Jimmy, spreading his arms wide. He won't let them kill the beast that fought so bravely to save him.

"I'll shoot you if you don't get out of the way!" yells the man. Jimmy sees that the man means it and throws himself down onto the grass. He hears a volley of shots and a howl of pain. Heart in his mouth, Jimmy turns to see both wolves running; the grey is making for the trees while the silver wolf is limping away over the lawn towards the lake. There is no sign of Mr Furey.

The men are too intent on reloading their guns to pay any attention to Jimmy Twigg. He slips to his feet and runs once more, dodging behind the men and into the trees on the far side of the lawn.

Chapter 15 - Lady Charlotte Vesper

Lady Winter collapses into a chair by the fireplace, quivering and blinking in shock. She is a small woman in her late forties, her greying hair tied back with a ribbon to keep it flat under her lost wig. Her thick make up is smudged and streaked with tears, her silk dress is torn and she is covered in a fine scatter of plaster dust.

"What shall become of us?" she says. "What is the world come to when murdering robbers defile our homes." She puts her face in her hands and begins to sob.

Ruby takes in the splendour of the room; the silk covered bed, the rich carpet, the golden wallpaper and the fine paintings in gilt frames. From the moment that she learned how Lord Winter made his money Ruby has hated this place. Even so, Lady Winter casts such a forlorn figure that she can't help feeling a little sorry for her.

Ruby goes to stand beside Lady Winter's chair. "You're safe now," she says. "The robbers won't dare to come back, not now that your husband's men are after them."

"They have laid waste to our house. We shall have go to live in the country while the damage is repaired," sobs Lady Winter. "The Sussex house is so vast and draughty - we shall all die of pneumonia."

"You have another house?" asks Ruby incredulously. How can this silly woman sit and cry about her future when she owns two enormous mansions? The poor of

London are lucky to have a roof over their heads to keep off the snow.

"One simply has to have a country place," sniffs Lady Winter. "London is so beastly in the summer."

Ruby remembers who she is pretending to be. The imaginary Lady Charlotte Vesper would probably not be shocked at the idea of someone owning more than one house. She nods her head and does her best to smile.

There comes a rifle shot from outside the window, followed by shouting and a volley of gunfire.

"Lord save us!" shrieks Lady Winter. "We are under attack."

Ruby goes to the window, lifts aside the curtain and looks out over the frost covered lawn. A group of men with lanterns are running towards a frozen lake. A four footed shape flits into the trees and the men follow. An eerie howl rings out into the night.

"What was that?" gasps Lady Winter

"It sounded like a wolf," says Ruby with a shiver. She has not heard a sound like that since the Witch Wolves came to Bascome Valley.

"This night is the strangest I have ever known," gasps Lady Winter, putting her hands back over her face.

The bedroom door bursts open and the young maid in the green dress rushes in. She sees Ruby standing at the window with her pistol and halts in her tracks.

"Emily," says Lady Winter. "Thank goodness. Is there any news of the robbers?"

Seeing that Ruby is not about to shoot her, Emily runs to Lady Winter and kneels on the carpet in front of her. She is tall and pretty but, like all the women at the ball, her face is heavily made up, giving her the look of a porcelain doll. Ruby guesses that she is only couple of years older than her; sixteen or seventeen.

"Are you alright, My Lady? Are you hurt? When I heard that the chandelier had fallen I couldn't believe it."

"I am uninjured," says Lady Winter. "Thanks to Lady Vesper. She saved my life."

"Oh my!" Emily looks up at Ruby and forces a smile. "But your dress, My Lady. It is ruined. I must help you change."

"Don't fuss," says Lady Winter." What I need is a stiff drink."

"Yes, My Lady. I've a tray ready."

Emily bobs a curtsey and leaves the room without giving Ruby a second glance.

"A lovely girl. Very attentive. But she has a tendency to get a bit above her station," says Lady Winter. "Poor dear, she is the niece of a distant relative. No hope of a good marriage, I'm afraid. But she keeps the other servants in order."

Lady Winter's voice is quite loud enough to be heard out in the corridor. Ruby feels herself sailing into treacherous waters. Lady Winter's petty spitefulness makes her skin crawl. Smiling politely and saying nothing seems to be her only option.

   Emily returns, carrying a large silver tray with a decanter of brandy, two glasses and a plate of brightly coloured cakes. She sets the tray down on the table at Lady Winter's side and pours her a drink.

"Come and sit with me, Lady Vesper," says Lady Winter, waving Emily away. "Have some brandy."

Ruby takes the seat on the other side of the fire. Lady Winter drinks her brandy down in one gulp and puts out her glass for Emily to refill. Ruby sips slowly, in what she hopes is a Lady-like manner, trying hard not to choke.

"Your dress is torn," says Lady Winter to Ruby. "We must find something else for you to wear in the morning."

"You are very kind," says Ruby. "But I have a carriage waiting."

"I will not hear of you leaving tonight," commands Lady Winter. "Not with those murdering bandits still at large. I am sure that we can find a room for you." She turns to Emily. "Have Sheridan prepare a bed for Lady Vesper and find a dress for her. One of the new ones that we bought for you last week would do well. You are a similar size, I think?"

"Yes, My Lady," says Emily. She curtsies to Lady Winter but as she turns to leave the room she gives Ruby a look of pure hatred. She will have to be careful of Emily.

"I should go and speak to my coachman," says Ruby. "He has been waiting out in the cold all night."

"I will send Emily to see to it," says Lady Winter. "Now, Lady Charlotte - I must call you by your first name, my dear, for we are going to be the best of friends." Lady Winter pours herself another large brandy and takes a swig. "I need distraction, otherwise I think I shall simply expire on the spot from the sheer terror. Tell me about yourself. Tell me how you came to England? Forgive me, but you do not seem Italian. Your accent is hard to place . . ."

Ruby has been dreading this moment. To tell the truth is out of the question, so she must spin a lie. Beneath the slightly dotty exterior lady Winter is clearly quite a shrewd individual but Ruby suspects that she might fall for a wild, romantic tale.

"My father was an Italian nobleman," begins Ruby. "He eloped with my mother when she was eighteen and I was born soon afterwards. He took her to live in his palace in Italy but when I was twelve years old my parents were lost at sea. Their ship sank in a storm off the coast of Egypt and all on board were drowned." Ruby manages a look of genuine sorrow here, remembering the loss of her own mother. "I was brought up by my Italian Uncle and an English governess. My uncle was kind but he was an awful gambler and before long he had lost the entire family fortune. When the estate was sold I used what little money I had left to come to London and search for my mother's family."

Ruby looks down at her hands. It strange to act a part like this - terrifying and exciting at the same time; she finds herself rather enjoying it. She glances up to see what effect her story is having and sees that Lady Winter's eyes are brimming with tears.

"My mother's family had disowned her and they had no wish to know me." Ruby sighs. "l have taken lodgings in London and when my funds run out I plan to become a missionary. I would love to see Africa."

"My dear child," says Lady Winter, dabbing her eyes with a handkerchief. "What a life you have had."

"Do not concern yourself about me," says Ruby. "I grew up without a mother and I am accustomed to looking after myself. I shall make my way in the world somehow."

Lady Winter's face breaks into a sudden smile.

"I have an idea," she says, clapping her hands. "A most capital idea! You shall come and live with me and be my companion. I have Emily, of course, but she is such a shrew. I shall introduce you to all the best people and we shall find you a nice young man to marry. Not a Navy man - I wouldn't wish that on anyone." Lady Winter laughs as she pours herself another large brandy, spilling a good deal of it onto the table. "When I think of the things I have had to put up with." She takes the brandy down in one breath and gives Ruby a flushed smile. "My husband is a wonderful man. But you must never marry a sailor, that is my advice. You are a pretty thing and I am sure that you have several suitors already?"

"Not really," Ruby blushes and looks down into her lap, pretending to be shy.

"I shall take you under my wing," says Lady Winter. She reaches over and pats Ruby's hand, then passes her the plate of cakes. "Have one of these, they are quite wonderful."

Ruby takes a marzipan cake and eats it slowly. By the time Lady Winter sobers up in the morning she may be less friendly. And there is Squire Colby to consider. Is he still at Winter Hall? Ruby doubts that Lady Winter's newfound affection for her will be enough to protect her against him.

Chapter 16 - Hunted

She leaps away over the frosty grass, her terror of the guns winning out over the agony that slams up her right fore-leg each time it hits the ground. They have put one bullet in her already and she won't be able to run for long.

More shots ring out and she hears the hiss of the bullets as they whip past her ears. She hears the shouts of the men and the drum of their boots on the frozen earth.

They are hunting her.

She veers away into the safety of trees. The bullet wound in her side burns like fire but she will not die from it. The injured leg is more dangerous; she needs to be able to run if she is to have any hope of escaping.

It was foolish to challenge Captain Ransome but it would have been her fault if the boy had died. After all, it was she who made the man into a werewolf.

Her memory of that night on the moors is hazy. She was newly changed and had no idea of her power. She left Captain Ransome by the stream, bleeding and barely alive. As his soul slipped toward death he must have been remade, as she had been.

Captain Ransome is a fearsome enemy but the one who she most fears - the one she most hates - was at Winter Hall as well; she scented him there. She will show no mercy to Squire Colby when she catches him.

Wolf rage consumes her and she howls her fury and sadness to the moon.

The cry sends a shiver down the spines of the hunting men, who halt and exchange nervous glances.
"The beast is alone and it is injured," growls Lord Winter. "Are you going to stand like cowards or help me hunt it down?"

The sounds of men crashing after her through the trees brings her to her senses. She lets go of her rage and pushes on.

The going is harder now. The wild burst of energy that carried her away from the guns has faded and the strength has gone out of her ruined leg, forcing her to limp forward on only three.

She needs somewhere to hide.

Her mind is stronger than it was when she was first changed. She is wiser now and she has learned to control her urges - sometimes. Wolf and human co-exist inside her, neither one master, neither one tamed. Right now, her wolf-self wants to find a dark place to curl up and lick her wounds but the human in her knows that there is no safety so near to Winter Hall. If the men do not catch her soon then they will fetch dogs, and there will be no hiding then.

She catches the scent of a fox and follows its trail into the bushes. She wriggles under a fence and through a thorny hedge. The men will struggle to follow a path like this. If she can only keep moving then there is a chance that she will live to see the dawn.

She passes the fox's den. She scents the creatures huddled down in the earth and wishes that she might creep down and join them. She limps on, through a beech wood and under a fence at the edge of a frozen field. A dog begins a frenzy of barking and she scents the rough stink of a farmyard. Away over the fields she sees the rising smoke of London.

Where can she go? There is no place in the land ahead where she could hope to hide. She lays down in a hollow between the tree roots, closes her eyes and rests her aching body.

A flurry of wings snaps her awake. She opens her eyes to see a sparrow perched on the frosty ground in front of her. He bobs his head and lofts up again, flying in a tight circle before darting away over the field. He lands on a frozen hummock of earth and turns to look back at her.

She has walked in the Twilight Land and she knows the taste of Faerie magic. She understands that the bird is not really a bird.

Limping and weak with pain, she follows where the Faerie sparrow leads, through shadowed hedgerows and over iron hard fields. She limps on, following the fluttering shape past outlying farms into the dark alleys of the sleeping city. Dogs growl and whine as she passes but she hardly hears them. The city is the last place that she should be going but she trusts in the bird.

By the time she reaches Star Alley she can barely stand. She slumps down on the doorstep of the pawnbroker's shop and lies still. The sparrow flies up to the window and taps on the glass with its beak.

Solomon Phoenix gasps when he sees the wolf stretched out on his doorstep. He has seen wolves before; he remembers the terror of them as they hunted him and his brother through the forests of Umbria. But that was long ago, and this wolf is not like those others. Fine limbed and silver grey, lying helpless on the door step, it is like a creature from a fairy tale. The old man also has the gift of True Sight, and from the corner of his eye he catches a glimpse of the other shape inside the wolf. He takes a step back and puts his hand on the door handle.
"Werewolf," he whispers, trying out the word for size. The name seems a good fit.
The haze of mist at the creature's muzzle tells him that it is still alive.
"What has brought you to my door?" he mutters. Wonder and curiosity win out over fear and he steps forward to kneel at the wolf's side.
The creature is badly hurt. Its foreleg is bloody and the flesh is torn down to the bone. There is a gash on its neck and a bullet wound in its flank.
The sparrow lands on the step beside the wolf and puts its head on one side.
"Good evening, Master Sparrow," says Solomon Phoenix."Is this your doing?"
The sparrow gives a chirrup and flaps its wings.

The old man puts a tentative hand onto the wolf's neck. There is a heartbeat, but it is faint. He leans down and whispers into the wolf's ear

"If you mean me no harm, then you are welcome in my house."

The wolf's eyes flick open and Solomon Phoenix sees no malice in them, only a tameless loneliness.

"Can you walk a few steps? I have a warm hearth to rest beside and medicine for your wounds."

She heaves herself painfully up onto three legs and follows Solomon Phoenix inside.

Chapter 17 - The Broken Crown

The moon has set and a thick blanket of clouds cover the stars. In the hut beside the gate of Bonehill burying ground the night-watchman slumbers in a chair. He does not hear the iron gate creak open but his little dog pricks up his ears and gives a low growl.

The watchman's eyes snap open and he stumbles to his feet.

"Who's there? Grave robbers?"

Grabbing up his stick, the watchman steps to the door and pulls it open, the dog at his heels.

A tall figure in a dark cloak stands at the gate.

"What's your business?" asks the watchman.

The hooded figure raises his head and the watchman meets Josia Colby's cold, grey eyes.

"Go back inside," says Josia Colby. "Go back to sleep and forget that you ever saw me."

The watchman blinks and nods and turns away but the dog stays at the door, baring its teeth and snarling. Josia Colby mutters a word under his breath that sends the beast scampering back to hide under his master's chair.

Josia Colby passes between the huddled grave stones until he reaches the place where the shadows lie deepest. On the site of the ancient plague pit there is a gap in the night. Josia Colby whispers into the emptiness and steps through the darkness into another place.

There are gravestones in this shadow city, and a path leading down to a rusting gate. The fields beside the burying ground are barren and the tumbledown houses at the road side are dark. It is deathly cold but there is no frost upon the ground.

The sorcerer walks out onto Knucklebone Lane, down Plague Street and Maggot Alley. The houses are broken and old. The mud and plaster have fallen from the walls, leaving only the bleached bones of buildings. A breath of wind might knock them down, but there is no wind here. There are no sleepers lying in the rotting beds and no rats scuttling in the gutters. There is no stink of human filth; only ankle deep dust and the dry scent of death.

A pale face watches from an upstairs window but the shade forgets the sorcerer as soon as he passes.

The streets wind down through the shadow city toward a dry river bed, past ghost houses and broken spires. In the distance rises a tower, tall and dark as the void between the stars. There is something so grim and terrible about the tower that it causes even Josia Colby to shudder.

He crosses the Desolate Market and comes to the inn. The rotted sign above the front door shows a crown and a white rose. The crown is broken and the white rose is withered.

He steps inside, into a darkness so deep he has to wait for his eyes to adjust.

She sits on a stool by the empty fire place, her sword on her knees. Her pale face is cruel and her eyes are dark. Her hair, her armour and cloak are jet black and around her neck is a rusted circlet of iron.

"Speak, mortal," she says. "I cannot linger for long in this accursed place."

"It must irk you to be so tightly bound by Queen Mab's power," says Josia Colby.

In the blink of an eye she is on her feet, her sword slicing through the air to halt a hair's breath from his throat. Her free hand grips his arm and twists it so that he is forced to kneel before her.

"You have cheated death for too long," she hisses. "It would be the work of a moment to dissolve the charms that keep your soul tethered. I am minded to feed upon you and be done with it."

Josia Colby feels her draw the strength from his body and the space of a heartbeat he is an old man again, bent and weak.

"If you destroy me then you will loose your chance of freedom," he gasps.

"We do not bargain with mortals. We are the Furies - we are the reapers of souls."

The sorcerer has not felt weakness like this since the night that he first drank the elixir. His name was Nathanial Colby and he was on the brink of death. He has remade himself since then and taken the name of his imaginary son, Josia, but he is the same man.

Terror and despair grip his throat but he fights them back. He must show no hint of weakness; strength is the only thing that the Furies understand.

"Why did Lord Ruin send a servant?" he says. "Is he trying to insult me?"

The rage-light in her eyes is awful to behold. Josia Colby feels his heart slow and a deathly chill grip his body.

"I am Torment," she says. "Mock me again and you will learn the true meaning of my name."

"I come to parley," whispers the sorcerer, the words drawn from his closing throat with the very last of his strength. "I come to forge a pact that will set us both free. With your help I can make an end to Queen Mab."

Torment snarls. She lets go Squire Colby's arm and he falls to the floor.

  The sorcerer's heart beats strong again and he takes a gulping breath.

"You presume a great deal," says Torment. "How could you to succeed where we have failed? To overthrow the Faerie Queen? The idea is beyond impudence."

"I have unravelled the secrets of Queen Mab's magic," says the Squire Colby. He can feel his strength returning but he remains on his knees. "Soon I will have a key to the gates of Faerie and the lost jewel from Queen Mab's crown. Once I wield the Faerie Star Queen Mab will have no choice but to kneel."

"And then?"

"I shall command her to release you from your bonds."

"You underestimate Queen Mab's pride. She will never agree to set us free."

"If she refuses then I shall destroy her. Once Queen Mab is gone her enchantments will be nought but dust."

Torment gazes down at the sorcerer. He keeps his face to the floor, watching her with hooded eyes.

"What aid do you seek from the Furies?"

"I ask for the benefit of your wisdom and for your protection," says Josia Colby. "When I summon Queen Mab I must bind her with a spell. It will require all of my art and strength to do this and for that instant I shall be vulnerable. The Furies are the most feared warriors in all the Nine Worlds. If you are at my side as I weave my snare about Queen Mab then no one will dare hinder me."

"Your scheme cannot work," says Torment. "We cannot pass into Faerie, nor can we walk in the Waking World."

"What of the crossing places where the Faerie roads and the Lychways meet?"

"They are few."

"Tell me of a such place and I shall open a path for you."

"A sacrifice must be made to open the way. A life must be stolen."

"Of course."

Torment gazes off into the darkness.

"There is a place where a Faerie path and a death Road cross," says Torment. "Between the Long Man's Gate and the Widow's Well is a track that we might walk, for a short span of mortal time." She raises her sword to the sorcerer's throat "Call us to the Widow's Well and we will come. Betray us and your suffering will have no end."

Chapter 18 - Escape from Winter Hall

Ruby is adrift in an ocean of shadows. A canopy of pale pink silk billows over her like a sail, caught in the light of the rising sun. Away in the distance glitter a field of golden flowers.

She hears the click of a fire flint and a flare of light dispels her dream. Flames crackle and she turns her head to see a hunched figure silhouetted against the glow of a fire. The girl stands up and knocks soot from the palms of her hands. She is dressed in a cream coloured dress with a white pinafore and hat. She is thin faced and small and looks about Ruby's age, thirteen or fourteen,

Ruby remembers; she is at Winter Hall, in the bedroom with the golden lotus flower wallpaper. Her name is Lady Charlotte Vesper.

The maid picks up a wicker basket from the fireplace and turns to the door. She sees Ruby watching her and gives a start of surprise.
"So sorry, My Lady," she says, lowering her gaze. "I didn't mean to wake you. I was just lighting your fire." The maid curtseys, keeping her eyes on the floor. "Is there anything else that you need, My Lady?"
"Can you tell me what time it is?" asks Ruby.
"Just after seven thirty, My Lady," says the maid, raising her eyes timidly.
Ruby had planned to be up before dawn, searching for the diamond. She had hoped to discover it and be off before anyone was awake. It was a wishful plan. Time to make a new one.

Ruby sits up. She is wearing the silk nightdress that she found waiting for her on the bed. Her dress has gone from the back of the chair and she can see no sign of her shoes.

"Do you know where my clothes have gone?"

"They've been taken for mending, My Lady," says the maid. "I have cleaned your shoes." She points to the shoes, standing by the door. "There's new dresses in the wardrobe, all from Lady Winter. She says you're to have any of them that you like."

"What's your name?"

"Verity, My Lady?"

"There's no need to call me My Lady," says Ruby. "My name is Charlotte. I won't mind if you talk to me like a normal person."

"Yes, My Lady." Verity blinks and frowns. Ruby grins and Verity smiles back.

"I'm supposed to address everyone by their proper title. Lady Winter is quite strict about it."

"I understand," says Ruby. She looks around the room. There seem to be great number of wardrobes and cupboards. "Can you show me where the clothes are?"

"Yes, My Lady." Verity heads to a large wardrobe with swirling gold leaf patterns on the doors. She opens the wardrobe doors goes to draw back the curtains and let the day in.

Ruby slips out of bed and finds an array of clothes; mostly dresses in various shades of green. She runs her hand over the fine silk and taffeta. The dresses are utterly impractical but very beautiful. No wonder Emily was so angry at having to give them up.

At the far end of the line Ruby finds a riding outfit consisting of a white chemise, an embroidered red jacket and a long red dress.

"Would you like me to dress you, My Lady?" asks Verity.

No one has dressed Ruby since she was six years old. She shakes her head.

"I can manage," she says. She sees Verity's worried look and realises that she has made another mistake. There are so many rules to being a Lady, most of them quite strange. "I don't suppose you know where I might get some breakfast?"

 Verity smiles:

"Breakfast is served in the dining room from eight o'clock. Or I could bring something to your room, if you prefer?"

Eating breakfast in a place like this is bound to involve all sorts of unspoken rituals. Besides that, Ruby wants to avoid the other guests as much as possible.

"Please bring my breakfast up here."

"Yes , My Lady," says Verity, curtseying and scurrying away to the door.

Soon all the servants will know that Ruby is no Lady - that's if Emily hasn't told them already. She must try harder to stay in character.

  The riding dress is a good fit and the jacket is loose enough to leave room for the pistol, stuffed into the waistband of the dress. In a box at the bottom of the wardrobe Ruby finds a pair of heeled riding boots. They are stiff and unworn and Ruby has just managed to get them on when Verity comes back with a huge silver tray. She sets it down on the table by the window, draws back the chair and stands with her eyes lowered, clearly waiting for Ruby.

"Thank you, Verity," says Ruby, doing her best to take her seat in an elegant manner.

Verity pours tea and lifts the silver covers off a series of dishes. There is enough here for several breakfasts; scrambled eggs, smoked fish, bacon, sausages, butter, marmalade and toast.

"What would you like first, My Lady?" asks Verity. Ruby isn't sure that she'll be able to eat with Verity standing at her elbow.

"I can serve myself," says Ruby."But while I am breakfasting, might you go and find my coachman and ask him to come and see me."

"Yes, My Lady. I'll take a message, of course," says Verity, looking more worried than ever. "But coachmen and outside staff are not allowed into the house, not in the normal run of things. Lady Winter won't hear of it."

"Of course," says Ruby, giving Verity what she hopes is a reassuring smile."If you could tell him to make my coach ready."

   Once the nervous maid has gone Ruby turns to her breakfast. She hasn't eaten anything apart from a tiny marzipan cake since she left Hawkins Yard and she is ravenous. She finishes the scrambled eggs, toast and bacon and is just beginning on the sausages when there is a soft knock at the door.

   Emily enters the room without waiting for a reply. She comes to stand next to Ruby's table and looks down at the red riding dress with her lips set in tight line.

"Lady Winter le cheide di farla visita nella sua stanza, quand e conveneitne," she says.

Ruby gives Emily a blank look. Too late, the answer comes; Emily must be speaking Italian.

A look of triumph flickers over Emily's face. It is gone in an instant but Ruby sees the danger of it: Emily knows for certain now that Ruby is an imposter.

Ruby remembers enough of her table manners not to talk with her mouth full. She puts her fork down slowly and places her hands carefully in her lap, giving herself time to think as she swallows the last of her breakfast.

"It is very kind of you to try and make me feel at home," says Ruby, smiling sweetly up at Emily. "But am in England now, so we shall speak English."

"Of course, My Lady," says Emily.

As Ruby has no idea what Emily said, it seems best to ignore it and wait to see what happens next. She turns away, takes a sip of tea and looks out over the garden.

The early sun is glittering on the frosty grass and the lake is shrouded in a haze of silver mist. Away in the distance the spires of London rise into a clear blue sky.

Ruby unfolds her napkin and dabs at her mouth, cleaning away some imaginary crumbs. She feels Emily's eyes on her the whole while but she does her best to appear at ease.

"What was it that you wanted, my dear?" asks Ruby, turning back to look up at Emily, as if she had forgotten that she was there.

"As I said, My Lady," says Emily, smiling coldly. "Lady Winter requests your company in her room. When it is convenient."

Ruby smiles. The act must continue. There is no other way.

"I have finished my breakfast," she says."Once you've cleared away you may take me to Lady Winter's chamber."

Emily's hate filled expression does not change.

"Very good, My Lady." Emily reaches out to tidy the breakfast things."A gentleman by the name of Josia Colby was asking after you," she says. Ruby's does her best to make no reaction but she cannot stop the slight catch of breath.

"I met a man named Colby at the ball last night," says Ruby. "He seemed a most unpleasant individual and he was certainly not a gentleman."

"He told me that he knew you from Cornwall," says Emily. "I told him that couldn't be possible, as you had only recently arrived in England, but he was most insistent."

"He is mistaken," says Ruby. She straightens her back and fixes Emily with an implacable glare. She focuses her hatred of Squire Colby into something ice cold and deadly."You have no place speaking to me that way. If you mention that man to me again then I shall take it as a sign of insolence. "

Emily holds Ruby's gaze for a moment before lowering her eyes.

"Very good, My Lady."

"You needn't worry," says Ruby softly."I do not plan to stay long at Winter Hall and I have no intention of attempting to replace you in your mistress's affections."

Emily's expression manages to convey relief, hatred and suspicion, all at the same time.

"None of us will be staying at Winter Hall," she says sniffily. "The whole household will be moving back to Sussex. Lady Winter has been most upset by the attempt on her life."

"When will she be leaving?"

"This afternoon."

"Then you had best take me to her at once."

"Yes, My Lady."

The house is bustling with activity. Servants are running everywhere, carrying breakfast trays, bundles of sheets, trunks and suitcases. When they see Ruby and Emily approaching they stop whatever they are doing and stand with their eyes lowered until they have passed. Ruby finds it unsettling to be treated this way but when she takes a sideways look at Emily the girl has a look of enjoyment on her face.

"Lady Charlotte, what a tonic it is to see you!" says Lady Winter.

Lady Winter is dressed in a canary yellow dressing gown. Her face has been made up for the day and her hair is pinned back, ready for the wig that stands ready on its silver stand. There are six servants in attendance; one holds a selection of petticoats and

123

corsets, a second a yellow silk dress, while a third is busy dusting the wig with silvery white powder . The remaining three maids are busy packing clothes and shoes into large travelling trunks.

The early sunlight glints on the broad golden stripes in the wallpaper, giving the room the look of a great gilded cage. The whole house feels like a trap to Ruby, a cage built on petty selfishness and injustice. Lady Winter is caught fast, her servants too. For Ruby, the cage door stands open, but she cannot leave yet.

"It is too awful," says Lady Winter. "I simply cannot remain in this house a moment longer. I am certain that the whole place is about to collapse on top of us. My husband assures me that we are safe but when I remember how close I came to death last night!" Lady Winter puts her hands up in a gesture of despair. "My dear, you must come with us to Elm Hall. It will be frightfully dull but we shall have to make the best of it. The hunting is good, they say. I can't stand all that out-doorsey stuff myself, but you look seem like a healthy sort of girl." She looks Ruby up and down and smiles. "That outfit suits you well, doesn't it Emily?"

"Yes, My Lady," says Emily stonily.

It seems that Emily has not yet managed to poison Lady Winter against Ruby but it will happen soon enough. Josia Colby will see to that.

"And now there is the packing to be done," sighs lady Winter, throwing herself down in a chair. "Such awfully hard work."

Two more maids come in to join the three already packing up Lady Winter's things. The maid with the corsets takes a step forward but Lady Winter waves her aside with a dismissive gesture. She turns to the gold encrusted dressing table and bends over a red velvet box. She lifts the lid and Ruby sees a flicker of light.

"I shall keep my diamond with me," says Lady Winter, lifting the Faerie Star on its broken chain. "My husband wants the necklace sent back to London to be repaired but I cannot bear to be parted from it."

Caught in the sunlight, the Faerie Star is even more beautiful than ever. The air in the room seems to sparkle. The maids all stop what they are doing and turn to gaze in wonder. Even Emily is entranced. The sunlit moment stretches on until it seems that the whole world has fallen under the spell of Queen Mab's diamond.

Ruby gazes at the Faerie Star, her mind running ahead of her. She has her pistol. She could take the jewel right now. If she locked Lady Winter and her servants into the bedroom then she would have a good chance of making it to the stables before the door was forced open again. But Ruby has no idea of the way to the stables and there is no way to telling if Tom will be ready to ride away when she gets there. She will have to wait a little longer.

Ruby pulls her eyes away from the diamond to find Emily watching her with a calculating expression. How much did Josia Colby tell the horrid girl? Has she guessed Ruby's thoughts?

"They say that it is cursed," says Lady Winter dreamily. "But it hardly seems possible. " She sighs and places the necklace gently back into its velvet box. "There shall be no reason to wear it in Sussex but I like to look at it. It is a most splendid thing." Lady Winter turns to Emily. "Fetch the strongbox. I want the diamond to be well secured for the journey."

Lady Winter nods to the waiting maids and they come forward and begin the process of dressing her. Ruby turns away and pretends to study the paintings on the wall, all the while watching Emily out of the corner of her eye. She sees Emily take out a leather covered box fitted with a heavy lock. The red velvet jewel case is placed into a hidden compartment at the bottom of the strong box and a collection of other jewel cases are placed on top. Emily then locks the box with a key which she hangs on a silver chain about her neck.

"Will you accompany me to breakfast, my dear?" says Lady Winter. It does not feel like a request.

"Of course, Lady Winter," says Ruby. "But I wonder if I might go and talk to my coachman first. It will only take a moment."

"There are so many things that you have to learn, Charlotte," says Lady Winter tartly. She has risen to her feet again and the three maids are fussing around her, trying to fit her yellow dress over her corset. "One does not talk to these people in person. It is simply not the way we do things in England."

Emily gives a smirk of satisfaction at Ruby's mistake.

"Of course, Lady Winter," says Ruby."I am a complete innocent when it comes to the manners of

126

my own country and I am most grateful for kind guidance. But if I am to accompany you to Sussex, I must send my man to my lodgings in London to fetch my personal things. On this occasion might it not be best if instructed him personally, to avoid mistakes?" "Oh, yes - if you must," Lady Winter waves a hand at one of the maids packing her clothes. "Polly, take Lady Vesper to the stables."
The maid curtseys to Lady Winter and leads Ruby from the room.

   The strongbox holding the Faerie Star is locked but Ruby knows where the key is kept. She might manage to steal the box during the confusion of loading the trunks into the coaches, or at the disembarkation at Elm Hall? There is another possibility - a wild and foolish scheme that makes Ruby want to laugh out loud.

   They make slow progress through the house. As well as the rushing servants, the guests are awake and heading down to breakfast. The men all stop and bow to Ruby and the women curtsey. Ruby smiles back in return but moves swiftly on before any of them can start a conversation. As they pass the door of the dining room Ruby glances in. Guests sit at a long table, eating, drinking and laughing with a feast laid out before them that makes Ruby's opulent breakfast look meagre. A whole roast pig sits on a silver platter, along with dishes of fruit and fish.
  At the far end of the room Lord Winter stands beside an enormous fireplace, deep in conversation

with a tall man in a black frock coat. The man turns and Ruby locks eyes with Josia Colby.

It is the first time that Ruby has seen her enemy's face since she spared his life. He appears young but his hair is white and his eyes are full of ancient darkness. She feels the mesmeric power of his will reaching out to her across the crowded room and for a moment she is caught fast.

A servant walks between them, carrying a tray of drinks, and the connection is broken. Heart thumping, Ruby turns away and runs as fast as she can down the corridor. Polly gives a gasp of dismay and runs after her.

"Please, My Lady - wait for me!"

Ruby and Polly find Tom and Charlie sitting with the other coachmen at the stable yard gate. The men all jump up when they see Ruby and stand to attention, their hands behind their backs, eyes lowered. Tom glances up and winks. Charlie grins. Ruby notices Polly's cheek redden as she smiles back at Charlie.

"That will be all, thank you, Polly," says Ruby. "I can find my own way back to Lady Winter's room."

Polly gives Charlie a wistful look and heads sadly back to the house.

"Coachman, I should like a word with you," says Ruby

"Yes, My Lady," says Tom hoarsely.

Ruby does her best to fix Tom with a stern look.

"Where is my carriage?" she snaps."I ordered it to be made ready."

"Allow me to escort you, Lady Vesper," says Charlie, gesturing to the driveway. "Thomas will fetch the horses."

"Very good," says Ruby.

Ruby follows Charlie to the line of carriages parked under the trees. Charlie opens the carriage door for her and bows.

"What happened to you at the ball?" Ruby hisses.

"I'm sorry," says Charlie, looking down at his boots rather than meeting Ruby's eye. "After the chandelier fell and it was bedlam. I tried to find you -"

"It doesn't matter," says Ruby. "I know where the diamond is hidden and I've an idea how I can get it. Go and help Tom with the horses. Speak to the other coachmen and see if you can find out the route that Lord and Lady Winter will be taking to Elm Hill this afternoon. Be quick!"

Charlie nods and sets off at a trot toward the stables.

Ruby waits in the carriage, watching the front door of the hall with the pistol on the seat beside her. Acting the part of Lady Vesper is still their best hope of escape but once Squire Colby has turned Lord Winter against her things will be desperate. Perhaps they should just steal some fast horses from the stables and make a run for it? If Ruby were on her own she might chance it but Tom is a hopeless rider and Charlie Angel is worse. A hasty escape would also mean leaving Sid's carriage behind, which would be no way to repay him for his kindness.

The sun has not yet reached the driveway and the carriage is icy cold. Sid's old coat lies on the seat where Ruby threw it last night but she dare not put it on until she is certain that they are leaving. She hears the crunch of approaching boots on the gravel driveway and grabs up her pistol. The footsteps draw closer but it is only a group of gardeners, heading along the drive to start taking down the lanterns from the trees.

Tom and Charlie return a moment later with the horses. When they are hitched to the carriage Charlie's face appears at the window.

"All ready, My Lady," he grins.

"What did you find out?"

"Lady Winter's leaving this afternoon but his Lordship is staying on until next week. She'll be taking the Sussex Road."

Ruby looks past Charlie's shoulder to see the front door of Winter Hall swing open. Josia Colby steps out with Lord Winter and several of his men. Ruby slams her hand on the roof of the carriage.

"Go! Drive as fast as you can."

Charlie scrambles up beside Tom and the carriage pulls away.

Josia Colby is leaning down to whisper in Lord Winter's ear. Lord Winter nods and gestures to his men and three of them run toward the stables. The carriage is picking up speed along the drive but it cannot go fast enough for Ruby. She watches in horror as Lord Winter's men return, leading a string of horses. Once they have mounted up they will outpace the carriage in no time.

As the carriage slows at end of the drive Ruby sees a way to buy them some time. She leans out of the window and shouts up to Tom:

"Stop the coach."

Tom reins in the horses and Ruby jumps out.

"Throw down the wheel chain," she shouts.

Tom rummages under his seat and throws down a heavy sack. Ruby catches it, runs to the nearer gate and begins to heave it shut. The gate is heavy but with Charlie and Tom's help it soon swings closed. They have just pulled the second gate shut when a man in a blue coat comes bursting out of the gate house with a face like thunder.

"What are you playing at?" He yells

"There was a message from the house," says Charlie. "Didn't you get it? The gates are to be closed."

"I'm the Gate Keeper," says the man, pulling a battered grey horsehair wig out of his pocket and jamming it hastily onto his bald head. "I know my job. I've been told to keep and eye out for trouble but to leave the gates open for the guests to leave."

The gatekeeper stares at Ruby and Tom, who are winding the rusty chain around the central bars of the gate.

"What's that in aid of?"

"Lord Winter's orders," says Charlie. "We think the robbers might come back. You better fetch your musket."

Tom loops the last links of chain around the bars and Ruby slips the padlock on.

"Who are you to be ordering me about?" mutters the gatekeeper. "I ain't seen you before ."

"Lord Winter is on his way to check the gate right now," says Charlie, pointing down the drive. "You can ask him yourself."

Ruby glances up. The Squire and Lord Winter have mounted up in front of Winter Hall and the first of his men are already cantering up the drive. Ruby snaps the hasp of the padlock shut and turns the key.

"Better get your gun," says Charlie. "And make sure its loaded. Lord Winter will expect you to be ready."

"I'll use it on you if you're jibbing me," says the gatekeeper. He scowls and stomps away to the gatehouse.

"Back to the carriage," hisses Ruby. "I'll drive."

Charlie and Tom jump into the back of the carriage and Ruby scrambles up onto the driving seat. She stands up on the foot boards and takes up the reins in her right hand. She touches her left hand to the charm around her neck.

"Run for all you are worth!" she calls.

The horses hear her; they respond to her voice and the magic of the Kern and they break into wild gallop.

Lord Winter's roar of rage at finding his own gates locked against him is drowned out by the thunder of the carriage wheels. Ruby laughs as the wind takes her hair, while in the back, Tom and Charlie hold onto the seats for dear life.

They have stolen some time but it won't be long before Lord Winter's men get the chain off the gate. Ruby's plan is to find a place to turn off the road and hide but as she slows the carriage down to turn onto the London Road, Charlie sticks his head out of the carriage window.

"Turn off along the lane by the Inn," he shouts. "Follow it through the woods and we'll come out onto the road down to Holloway. It's slower than the Turnpike but we should be safe."

Ruby does as Charlie tells her. The carriage bumps its way down a muddy track, turns onto the lane at the far end, and they ride by winding roads, back through Holloway and Ring Cross, to Hackney.

Chapter 19 - The Return of Jack Shadow

Ruby folds the red silk riding habit and lays it on the bed. She needs her travelling clothes now; the breeches, the dark jacket and the black cloak. She pulls on her old riding boots and takes the scarf and hat from the peg on the wall. She loads her pistols and slips them into the leather strap over her chest.

Hawkins yard is quiet. The horses are all out working, Hannah and Katy are at the market and Sid and Seth are out dealing with a broken carriage wheel. Only Tom and Charlie are there to see Ruby off.

Tom hands Ruby the map that he has sketched for her.

"It shows the Sussex Road and the turn-off at Wytch Cross" he says. "Are you sure you don't want me and Charlie to come with you?"

"I have to ride fast," says Ruby. "And I'll need to go even faster once I've got the diamond."

"The coach will be guarded," says Tom.

"I know."

Ruby has no wish to come up against Lord Winter's men. She has a plan to distract them but the whole scheme depends on her finding the right place for an ambush. She has to reach Wytch Cross before sunset and scout out the road.

"I have to take this chance," she says. "Once the diamond is at Elm Hall it will be far harder to take."

Ruby takes the axe that Tom has wrapped in an old sack and straps it to the back of Dervish's saddle. She puts her foot in the stirrup and swings herself up.

"I'll be back by morning."
Tom and Charlie watch her ride out of the gate of Hawkins Yard.
"I still think we should go with her," says Tom.
"You can go," says Charlie. "But you'll not get me on a horse."
"We could borrow Mr Blake's trap."
Tom stops. Four men have appeared at the gate of the yard. They have clubs and pistols in their hands and they have thieves eyes; sizing up everything they see, guessing its worth and how hard it would be to carry off.

Ruby rides to Westminster. She crosses by the bridge and heads down to Kennington. She rides fast to Streatham, where she stops to let Dervish drink. A coachman is watering his horses at the same trough and takes Ruby for a young gentleman.
"Where are you bound?" he asks.
"Newhaven," says Ruby gruffly.
"Taking a ship?"
Ruby nods and turns away to check the girth straps on her saddle.
"It's not a road I'd like to ride alone," says the coachman. "The highwaymen on Thornton Heath are likely to take your horse off you."
Ruby puts her foot in the stirrup.
"They'd have to catch me first," she says. She grins at the coachman and Dervish springs away.

Thornton Heath turns out to be a desolate place, just right for an ambush, but the highway robbers are nowhere to be seen. The only sign of human life is a lonely cottage and a gallows beside a frozen pond. Ruby rides on as fast as she can, shaking off the memory of her own journey up the gallows steps on Reaver's Hill. She would have ended her life at the end of a rope if it hadn't been for Davey.

If Davey were here now then he would tell her that her plan is plain crazy. But Davey is not here; he is far away and the only way to get him back is to take the diamond. Ruby might have made light of it to Tom, but the thought of what she is about to do fills her with dread.

She urges Dervish on harder, letting the wind take her fear.

The miles blur past and they come, at last, to the Wytch Cross turnpike. Checking the map, Ruby turns aside and follows the road into the forest.

A couple of miles into the woods Ruby finds just the place; a low hill overlooking a dip where the road crosses a ford. She rides up the road on the far side of the river, far enough to find a forest track, perfect for an escape route.

Leaving Dervish to drink at the river, Ruby sets to work with the axe, weakening a dead tree on the bank. When the job is done, she mounts up and rides back up to the hilltop.

She has to wait for nearly an hour in the freezing wind, watching the sun sink toward the horizon. Several carts and coaches go by before she catches sight of a carriage with four outriders coming from the direction of Wytch Cross. There might be another guard inside the carriage but it is better odds than she'd hoped for.

She gallops Dervish down the hill and over the ford, where she dismounts and leads the chestnut mare into the trees.

"Wait here," she says. "I'll be back soon."

Dervish nuzzles Ruby's hand and gives a soft whinny.

The ford is shallow enough to cross on foot but the water rises over the tops of Ruby's boots. The cold bites deep and Ruby's hands are shaking as she pulls the axe from its hiding place. She brings the tree down with two swift chops and it falls just where she planned, blocking the ford. She covers the freshly cut tree stump in old leaves and crouches down in the bushes. Dusk is drawing in and her black cloak makes her all but invisible.

Ruby's teeth are chattering with cold, her heart is thumping and she has the familiar knot of panic in her belly. The terror of waiting before a robbery never gets any easier.

She takes a deep breath and wills her hands to stop shaking. When she left Cornwall, she thought that she would never have to do this again. She prays that her luck will hold, one last time.

The guards spot the tree and the coach comes to a halt. The mounted men take out their muskets and look warily about. They are no fools; a fallen tree in the road is an old trick of highway robbers.

"You'll have to get down and shift it," shouts the coach driver. "We'll lose too much time if we double back. It'll be dark soon."

"You shift it," shouts the nearest of the blue coated riders.

There follows a short and colourful argument, which is ended by Lady Winter sending Emily out to talk to the guards. The men dismount and, along with the coach driver, three of the guards wade out into the freezing water to drag the tree out of the way. The guard captain stands on the bank with his musket at the ready. He is supposed to be keeping watch but he is too busy shouting helpful insults at the men in the river to notice Ruby creeping out from her hiding place.

She goes to the tethered horses and ducks down to loosen the leather girth straps that hold their saddles on.

"Come on you lazy skulks," laughs the guard captain."Put your backs into it!"

There is loud splash as the coach driver slips and falls face first into the water. The other men roar with laughter and the coachman comes up for air, spluttering and cursing.

Under cover of the noise, Ruby runs back to the carriage. She crouches by the lead horse and peeps over its back at the men in the river.

The coach driver is standing on the far shore, shivering, but the three guards have got hold of the tree and are pulling it clear of the ford.

Ruby puts her hand onto the horse's neck.

"I need you to run for me," she whispers. "Wait for my word."

The horses are fine beasts, heavily made and strong. The lead horse lowers its head and snorts softly.

The tree slips down into the deeper water, the current lifts it and it drifts away downstream. Ruby leaps up onto the lead horse's back.

"Now," she hisses." Run!"

The four horses pull forward together, clattering down the road into the river, water flying from their hooves, turning to silver sparks in the light of the rising moon.

"Stop!" yells the captain of the guards.

He makes a grab for the carriage but it slips past him and he has to jump back to avoid being crushed under the wheels. The men in the river scatter, diving into the water to escape the rushing horses.

The carriage rolls up onto the far bank and the horses pull up the slope. Ruby turns to see the driver and two of the guards running after them. Back at the ford, the guard captain puts his foot in the stirrups of his horse and hauls himself up, only for the saddle to slip sideways and send him tumbling to the ground

The horses snort and strain, hauling the carriage on, and there are thuds and screams from inside as luggage and passengers are tumbled about. A window swings open and Emily sticks her head out:

"What on earth are you playing at?" She sees the carriage's empty driving seat and the masked figure astride the lead horse and gives a gasp of fear. "Oh Lord!"

They reach the top of the slope just in time. The nearest of the guards has his hands on the luggage straps at the back of the carriage but before he can climb aboard the horses kick forward into a gallop. The man falls and the horses race away over the level ground.

Ruby puts her fingers to her lips and gives a loud whistle. There is an answering whinny from the trees and Dervish appears, galloping out into the road to run along behind the carriage. The road takes a couple of turns before Ruby sees the track. She hauls the horses around and the carriage swerves into the trees.

The track is narrow but the ground is solid enough and Ruby urges the horses into a stiff gallop. The carriage races on, swaying and jumping as the wheels bounce over the rough ground. Branches swish over Ruby's back, sweeping off her hat. There are fresh screams from the back of the carriage and a series of thuds as the trunks strapped to the roof of the carriage come tumbling off.

The headlong flight ends when one of the carriage wheels hits a rock and shatters. The carriage lunges to one side and skids into a tree.

Ruby slips off the lead horse's back and looks about.

Two of the carriage wheels are broken and the horses are tossing their heads in indignation, pulling at their twisted traces. Dervish stands nearby, waiting patiently. The carriage horses are unhurt but Ruby can't leave them like that. She takes a knife from her boot and cuts the leather straps holding the horses into the shafts of the carriage.

There comes the drum of galloping hooves from the road and Ruby holds her breath to listen. The riders run on, just as she had hoped, but it won't be long before the men guess that they've been tricked and double back.

Ruby's hat is gone, her cloak is in tatters and there is a nasty gash on her forehead that drips blood into her eye. She wipes the worst of the blood away with her scarf and wraps it back over her face. She takes a pistol from her belt and knocks at the door of the coach with the heel of her boot.

"Come out ladies," she says, in as deep a voice as she can manage. "I mean you no harm. I only want to rob you."

There is a chorus of shrieking from inside the carriage. Ruby keeps her pistol ready as she pulls the door open.

The inside of the carriage is a chaos of tumbled trunks and cases, some of which have broken open, spilling lace petticoats and silk stockings in all directions. Lady Winter, Emily and Polly are huddled together in the far corner, their eyes wide with fear.

Ruby spots the strongbox jammed under the seat. Brandishing her pistol, she leans in and takes hold of the strongbox handle. Emily flinches back, Polly buries her face in her hands and Lady Winter stares blankly, her mouth opening and closing in a silent expression of terror. Ruby feels a stab of guilt a she remembers Lady Winter's kindness. Then she remembers Winter Hall, built upon the misery of slavery, and she remembers Davey, trapped in the Twilight Land.

Ruby hauls the strongbox out onto the ground.
"If you would be kind enough to give me the key to
this box," she says.

No-one moves. Ruby raises her pistol and Emily
moves forward, putting herself between Lady Winter
and Ruby.

"We will not assist you in your villainy," she says.
"You'll have to shoot me first."

"Lady Winter is lucky to have such a devoted
servant," says Ruby. "But I have no wish to kill you.
Why don't you give me the key that you wear about
your neck?"

"How did you know . . . ?" Emily's eyes widen. "It's
you!" She hisses. "The imposter! Josia Colby was
telling the truth."

Ruby's pistol explodes with a crack and Emily falls
back, screaming.

Ruby stows her used pistol, takes out a new one
and kicks open the lid of the strongbox. Shooting the
lock off the box was a desperate move, and it will
bring Lord Winter's men down on them all the
sooner, but it seemed easier than fighting Emily for
the key. Ruby tips the contents of the box onto the
ground and pulls open the hidden compartment. She
takes out the red velvet case, flicks it open far enough
to be sure the diamond is inside and slips it away into
her cloak.

"You'll hang for this," says Emily. "Whoever you are."

"You may call me Jack Shadow," says Ruby, with a
bow. She steps to Dervish's side, puts her foot into
the stirrup and leaps up.

Half way back down the road to ford, Ruby comes across the bedraggled coachman coming up the hill alone. The poor man is half frozen to death and he shrinks back in terror at the sight of the ragged, bloody faced rider with a pistol in her hand.

"Your mistress and her maids are unharmed," says Ruby."The coach is along the track up ahead. Do you have a fire flint?"

The man blinks and nods.

"Build a fire and dry yourself out. The broken carriage wheels should burn nicely."

The man stumbles away and Ruby kicks Dervish forward.

Ruby is giddy with relief; she can hardly believe that her wild plan has succeeded. She can feel the weight of the Faerie Star in the pocket of her jacket, thumping against her side as she rides.

They cross the ford and gallop back up the road towards Wytch Cross. She will ride the Turnpike back up as far as Croydon, then turn aside to confuse her pursuers. She'll try and find a barn to sleep in for an hour or so. Dervish is a strong horse but she can't gallop all the way back to Hackney tonight. Once Ruby is back at Hawkins Yard they can rest for a few days before setting off for Cornwall. Davey's freedom is within her grasp.

Chapter 20 - Betrayed

Dervish gives a shriek of terror and veers away into the trees. Ruby catches a glimpse of the beast in the road ahead. The wolf is as tall as a man, its coat the colour of wet ashes.

She flattens herself against Dervish's neck and holds on tight. Branches snap and scrape over her head and back, blinding her and ripping off her cloak. Sudden pain gashes along her arm and she looses her grip on the reins. She does her best to stay in the saddle but Dervish gives an unexpected sideways swerve and she is thrown off.

There is a slow, weightless moment filled with spinning trees and stars. Ruby feels the wind on her face and for an instant it as if she is flying. She hits the ground hard and feels her ankle twist under her, sending a white hot jolt of pain shooting up her leg. Her face slams into the mud and she tastes rotting leaves and blood. `

Terror pulls Ruby to her feet. The wolf is near - she can hear it crashing through the trees towards her. Her head is ringing and her left ankle gives way as soon as she puts her weight on it. Pain fells her and she sinks to her knees, fumbling for her pistol.

There is a crack of snapping branches and the wolf is there, towering over her, its teeth glittering in the moonlight, its stink choking her. This is no ordinary beast. Its sheer size marks it out as something otherworldly and there is a malicious intelligence in its eyes that makes Ruby's blood run cold.

The wolf lowers its head and paces forward with its hackles raised. Ruby turns her face away and pulls the trigger. The pistol explodes, pain jolts up her arm and the wolf leaps back into the trees.

Ruby glances down in shock at the smoking pistol. The hammer has snapped clean off and the breech is cracked open. The bullet must have jammed in the barrel. Ruby's hand is still stinging from the blast but her leather glove saved her from worse injury.

The wolf paces forward again. It glances down at the ruined gun and back up into Ruby's eyes, considering its options in a chillingly human way. It draws back its lips and makes a low growling sound that might be a laugh. Ruby pulls out her last pistol out and points it at the wolf's head.

"I'll not miss this time," she says.

If the wolf is a Faerie beast then it might prove hard to kill. Ruby aims for the wolf's left eye and steels herself to pull the trigger. She hates to fire at a living creature but if it comes at her again then she will have no choice.

The wolf growls and slinks back. Ruby pulls herself up against a tree and shuffles forward with her pistol raised.

"Run!" she shouts. "Before I put a bullet in you!"

The wolf gives a surly snarl and lopes off into the darkness.

She needs to find Dervish. The Faerie Star is safe in her pocket but she has to get away as soon as she can. Lord Winter's men will have realised the trick by now and will be riding back at any moment.

Ruby puts her fingers to her lips and whistles. The answering whinny is distant, somewhere away up the hill to the right. Dervish won't return to a place that stinks of wolf. Ruby will have to go after her.

She uses the torn remains of her scarf to bind up the gash in her arm. Her ankle is agony and she's pretty sure that its broken but there's no time to do anything about it; her riding boot will have to hold it for now. She checks and reloads her two remaining pistols, cuts a branch into a makeshift crutch, and heads up the hill, keeping a wary eye out for the wolf. Every step sends a blade of pain up her left leg but she pushes herself on, pausing only to whistle for Dervish.

She finds the chestnut mare standing in a clearing at the top of the hill, shivering and stamping with fear. She puts a hand on the horse's neck.
"Thank you for waiting," says Ruby. "We'll ride home together. I'll do my best to keep the wolf away."
Ruby has to climb onto a fallen tree to get up onto Dervish's back. It's an agonising process but she finally manages to get both feet into the stirrups. Her left foot can't take any weight and she hopes that she won't have to ride fast again.

The Sussex Road will be too dangerous now that she has lost her lead on Lord Winter's men. Tom's map doesn't give much detail but she should be able to find her way back to London if she heads north. If she keeps the moon behind her she should make it.

She has just found a decent track, heading in roughly the right direction, when the wolf comes at them again, lunging out of the bushes behind Dervish, snarling and nipping at the mare's legs. Dervish leaps into a mad gallop and Ruby grips tightly to the reins with one hand, pulling out a pistol with the other. She swings her arm back and fires but the beast jumps away and the bullet misses by a mile.

The wolf stays out of range but it keeps after them. On open ground Dervish would soon outrun the beast but they are on a winding forest track. Ruby can only hold tight and do all she can to keep Dervish from harm.

The track plunges down into a stream bed and up a muddy slope to a place where several paths meet. The wolf leaps up at Dervish, spooking the horse into veering away onto a narrow side path. The trees are packed too closely for Ruby to have any hope of taking another shot and the wolf runs nearer, driving Dervish wild with fear. The pain in Ruby's ankle is almost too much to bear - each jolt of the path sending a new wave of agony up her leg.

The path crosses another and Dervish is driven towards the right once again. At the next crossroads the wolf pushes Dervish straight on. The wolf is large enough to bring Dervish down any time it wants to but it seems content to chase. It seems to be steering them south, away from London.

How long they run for, Ruby cannot tell. Dark trees tumble past in a blur of moonlight and the horse thunders on. The pain in Ruby's ankle bites deeper and the wolf never falters in its chase, snapping at

Dervish's legs if she tries to stray from the course it has set for them.

Ever since Ruby took the Faerie Star her luck has failed her. She had not set much store by the stories of the diamond being cursed but now she can believe it. Will she die before she has a chance to take the jewel to Queen Mab?

Ruby buries her face in Dervish's neck, closes her eyes and calls on the power of the Kern to help them. The nightmare does not end but she feels a spark of renewed strength kindle in her heart. Far off in the wilderness of her memory she hears her mother's voice:

"Stay true, Ruby - stay true."

Ruby rides in a waking trance. Dervish lets the wolf drive her where it will and Ruby slumps down onto the mare's neck, trusting Dervish to carry her safely.

At long last, they break out onto open ground. There is no hope of trying to outrun the wolf; Ruby can feel Dervish weakening with every step, stumbling her way over the ploughed field. Dervish plods wearily on for a few steps, shudders and comes to a halt.

Ruby sits up in the saddle. She turns about and stares into the darkness but there is no sign of the wolf. Has the beast really gone this time? It makes no sense. Why would it drive them so deliberately just to let them go?

There is a hedge ahead, with a gate opening onto a lane.

"Just a little further," Ruby whispers, nudging the horse forward."We need a safe place to rest."

Dervish snorts wearily and walks out through the gate. The land falls away and the forest thins out into fields. There will be a barn somewhere down there, perhaps even a friendly farmhouse.

They have not ridden far when they meet someone coming along the lane; two men, leading a tall white horse. One of the men raises his head and shouts to her.

"Ruby!"

Is she dreaming? Can it really be Tom and Charlie.

"How on earth did you find me?" Ruby asks, as Tom and Charlie draw alongside her. "And where did you get a horse like that?"

The horse that Tom leads is a fine white stallion a hand or two taller than Dervish.

"We borrowed it," says Tom with a grin.

Charlie stands a little way behind Tom. He glances up at Ruby and gives her a thin smile but seems unwilling to meet her eye.

The wild ride has taken its toll on Ruby. Her body feels broken and her thoughts are muddled.

"We have to get back to London," says Tom.

"Soon," says Ruby. "I need some rest first. So does Dervish. I've hurt my ankle. I think it might be broken."

"There's no time," says Tom, his voice urgent. "We have to save Katy and Seth."

"What do you mean?"

"Mr Famish's men came, just after you left," says Tom. "We tried to fight them off." Ruby notices the bruise on her brother's face and a bloodied bandage on his arm. "They knocked me out and took Katy and Seth away."

This cannot be happening. How can Seth and Katy have been taken?

"Mr Famish took them to exchange for the diamond," says Charlie. "Josia Colby has promised Famish a King's ransom in gold if he can bring him the Faerie Star."

Tom flashes Charlie an angry look and his features blur. The moon catches in Ruby's eyes, dazzling her. When she looks back at Tom he is gazing back at her, earnest and concerned.

"I know what that diamond means to you," he says. "But Mr Famish says he'll kill Seth and Katy if we don't give it to him."

"It was that little rat, Jimmy Twigg, who sold you to Famish," says Charlie Angel.

Ruby has sworn to free Davey but she will not do it the price of her father and her sister's lives.

"Do you have the diamond?" asks Tom.

Ruby nods. It's getting harder to string her thoughts together. What is happening? She is dizzy and her eyes are heavy. This is more than exhaustion. Did she scramble her brains when she fell from the horse?

There is a shout from behind and Ruby turns to see a gang of men with lanterns running down the lane towards them.

"Famish's men," says Tom. "They must have followed us."

How did a gang of men on foot follow Tom and Charlie all the way from London? How did Tom and

Charlie find her? Did they ride together on that horse? Everything is wrong. Ruby shakes her head in an attempt to clear her mind.

"We'll have to make a break for it," says Tom, leaping up onto the white stallion's back

"Take Charlie up on Dervish," he shouts.

"She's worn out," says Ruby. "Your horse is stronger." The words die on her tongue as Dervish skitters back, her eyes rolling in panic.

The grey wolf is standing in the road ahead, blocking any chance of escape into the farmlands below. Tom's horse catches the wolf's scent and rears up, shrieking and snorting. Tom manages to stay in the saddle and brings the stallion's front hooves down again. Dervish is too exhausted to bolt and Ruby easily manages to rein her in.

She looks about for an escape route but the hedges lining the lane are too high to jump. There is no way that the horses will run toward the wolf. Their only hope is to gallop at Mr Famish's men and pray that they are not shot from their saddles.

The stallion is rearing again, doing all it can to throw Tom off. Ruby puts out a hand and pulls Charlie on behind her. Dervish might carry them both for a little while. She urges Dervish on up the road but the white stallion is turning about in a frenzy of terror, blocking their way.

"Give me the Kern!" says Tom. "I'll be thrown off otherwise." He puts out a hand to Ruby, desperately trying to control the horse with the other. "Please, Ruby! Just until we get away."

The Kern has hung around Ruby's neck ever since the day her mother put it there, ten years ago. It is the most precious thing that she owns - almost a part of her. But right now, Tom needs the kern more than she does; if the white stallion isn't brought under control then all is lost.

The stallion rears again and Ruby sees the panic in Tom's eyes. She loops the charm over her head and throws it to her brother. He shoots out a hand and grabs it out of the air.

"Ride!" shouts Ruby, turning Dervish's head up the lane.

Dervish stumbles forward. To make her gallop with two riders seems cruel but Ruby has no choice.

The whole world out of kilter. Is it the power of Loki's curse taking hold? Ruby's head is spinning, her vision blurring. She doesn't know how much longer she'll be able to stay in the saddle. All she knows is that they must get away up the lane.

Mr Famish's men have halted in a line across the road and they are preparing their rifles. It might already be too late.

"Come on!" calls Ruby.

She looks back over her shoulder but Tom is not there.

"There is no need to hurry," says a cold voice.

Ruby freezes, unable to comprehend what she is seeing. The man sitting in the back of the white stallion is not her brother, it is Squire Colby.

A wave of dizziness sweeps over her, so strong that she almost tumbles from the saddle. Too late, Ruby recognises the feeling of confusion; she has been enchanted.

Josia Colby looks down the lane towards the grey wolf. He makes a dismissive gesture with his hand and the ragged beast slinks off into the night. He turns and kicks his horse forward until he is level with Ruby.

"Your kindness has always been your greatest weakness," he says. "If I had tried to take the Kern from you by force then its power would have been broken. The only way for it to be passed on to me was as a gift, freely given."

Ruby opens her mouth to speak but her tongue will not move.

"I have a key to the gates of Faerie," he says, holding up the Kern. "All that I require now is Queen Mab's diamond." He slides the Kern into his pocket and puts out his hand. "The Faerie Star, if you please."

Ruby feels Charlie Angel shift his weight in the saddle behind her.

"Best do as he says," whispers Charlie. She feels the cold steel of a knife blade press up against her throat.

"Where's Tom?" asks Ruby.

"A simple charm was all it took to change my appearance," says the Squire. "You saved me a great deal of trouble by stealing the diamond. It is a fitting final act to the legend of the notorious Jack Shadow."

Ruby tries to turn and look at Charlie but he presses the knife up to her chin.

"Please don't make me hurt you," he says.

"You betrayed us," hisses Ruby."You were betraying us from the start."

"I'm a thief and a liar," says Charlie. "It's in my nature."

"Tom called you his friend."

"More fool him."

Charlie is doing his best to sound unconcerned but Ruby can hear the fear in his voice.

"You don't have to do this," says Ruby.

"I don't have a choice," says Charlie.

"Where is Tom? What have you done with him?"

"Your brother is safely under lock and key," says Josia Colby." Your sister and your father will be joining him soon. They will be kept as insurance, to concentrate your mind upon the task in hand."

"What task?"

"It is not your place to ask questions ," says Josia Colby. "You will die soon, whatever choice you make, but your compliance with my wishes will buy the lives of your family. That is all that you have left to bargain for."

Chapter 21 - Moonwolf

Lucy Cotton wakes. She is wrapped in a blanket and firelight is dancing over her closed eyelids. For a moment she wonders if she might be back home in her granny's cottage in Penzance? But this place doesn't smell like Granny's house. It has a strange, bitter scent, like burned metal.

Lucy sits up and looks about. She is in a windowless room, all made of stone. It is dry and warm, there is a beautiful red carpet on the floor and the walls are lined with bookshelves, their golden spines glowing in the firelight. There is a curtain over an opening in the wall and a silvery light chinking out from underneath.

The silver light draws Lucy forward like a magnet. She pulls the blanket around herself and goes to investigate. When she pulls back the curtain and sees what is on the far side she gives a gasp of wonder.

Down a short flight of steps is a narrow room with workbenches along the walls. The benches are littered with bottles and jars, lengths of twisted copper tubing, scrolls, books, fire blackened tools and crucibles. Standing on an iron frame at the far end of the room is a clear glass globe full of moonlight.

Lucy's feet carry her forward and she halts a couple of steps from the glass sphere. The silvery light fills her eyes, sinking into the weave of her bones. The wolf inside her wakes but it does not come rushing to the surface. Her wolf-self is soothed by the light, content to bask in its radiance.

There are colours inside the light and shapes that flicker and fade. Lucy sees her Granny, sitting by the fire, darning a patch onto a dress. She sees her little sister, Sophie, asleep in her attic bed. She sees the streets of Penzance and bobbing fishing boats and the starry sky over the sea. She sees the misty hills and forests of Faerie and she sees Davey Tachard, sitting enchanted at the feet of Queen Mab. She sees the winter woods of Sussex and she sees Ruby Gilbert with her hands tied to the saddle before her, sitting on a horse. Lucy sees Josia Colby riding ahead on a white stallion, holding the lead rope in his hand. She sees a crumbling stone well in a grove of rotting trees and she sees a crack in the edge of the world. In the darkness beyond the gap stand a host of cruel eyed warriors.

Lucy feels a hand on her shoulder and turns to see an old man smiling at her. She cannot remember his name but she knows that he is kind.
"Come away, child," he says.
Lucy follows the old man back into the study and he sits her in one of the chairs by the fire.
"Your injuries seem to have healed remarkably well," he says.
Lucy looks down at her bandaged arm. She lifts it and when she flexes her fingers she finds her arm strong and whole.
She remembers the battle with the grey wolf and the flight through the fields. She remembers the old man opening his door to her.

"Thank you, sir," she says. "I think I would have died if you hadn't taken me in."

"My name is Solomon Phoenix," he says. "And I am glad to have been of help to you." He watches her with his sharp, blue eyes. "The moon is up, but you are still human?"

"It is the silver light," says Lucy, looking back towards the curtain. "It keeps the wolf away."

"Luna's radiance can work great changes."

"Does this mean I'm cured?" she asks. "Am I freed from the curse?"

The old man shakes his head and smiles sadly.

"As long as you remain near the light you will retain your true shape but once you leave this house you will change again. The magic that made you a werewolf came from Faerie, not from this world."

"Must I go to Faerie to have it undone?"

"Perhaps."

Lucy remembers the visions that she saw in the glass and starts up from the chair.

"Ruby Gilbert is in danger," she says. "I have to find her."

All of a sudden the cosy room feels like a cage. Lucy turns about, her eyes wild. "Show me the way out - I have to go!"

Solomon Phoenix does not try to dissuade her. He sees the urgency in her eyes and he leads Lucy to the door of the study. They pass through his jeweller's workshop and up the stairs into the shabby little pawnbroker's shop.

Lucy runs to the door and reaches for the handle. Moonlight is pooling on the worn wooden boards at her feet and already she can feel the change coming. "You better lock the door."

"I do not fear you."

"Thank you." Lucy flashes him a smile and slips out, closing the door behind her.

The moonlight hits her full in the face and she falls to the cobbles, shaking and snarling.

When Solomon Phoenix opens the door, a few moments later, Lucy is gone.

Chapter 22 - Brock and Snout

The sparrow lands by the wall of the cottage and pecks at the ground.

"Here?" asks Brock.

The sparrow nods and gives a loud chirrup. Brock sniffs the air. The house smells bad. Cruel people live here and he does not wish to meet them.

"Let's get the job done quick and get out of here," he mutters, making an experimental scrape at the frozen earth.

"How far down?" he asks.

The sparrow ducks its head and flattens its wings onto the ground.

"Pretty deep?" Brock turns to Snout. "We better get digging."

Snout gives a snuffle of agreement and the two badgers shuffle up to the wall and set to work.

Once they get past the frozen surface layer the going gets easier. They work side by side, quiet and steady, their powerful claws cutting into the earth, pushing it back to be kicked out of the hole with their muscular back legs.

The badgers soon disappear out of sight behind a mound of freshly dug earth, on top of which the sparrow perches, keeping look out.

Tom wakes in darkness. He is in a cold place that smells of damp and rot. His hands are tied and his head feels as if it has been cracked open. The last thing he remembers is standing in Hawkins Yard, watching Ruby ride away.

What happened after that?

The agony dawns on him slowly.

The men came through the gate of the yard and Tom had hardly opened his mouth to challenge them when someone bashed on the head. The only other person there was Charlie Angel. The realisation hits Tom hard. He knew that Charlie was a rogue but he had thought he was his friend. The betrayal hurts far more than his bruised skull.

The lying scumbag had been plotting against them all along.

After a good deal of wriggling, Tom manages to stand up. He moves slowly, one step at a time, mapping out his prison. It's not a big place and he is the only thing in it. He finds the door but it is jammed shut, most likely locked from the outside. He puts his ear to it but he hears nothing.

Dejected, Tom slides down against the wall.

The scraping sound is faint at first but it gets steadily louder. It seems to be coming from the far wall. Tom creeps forward and hears distinct sound of digging, accompanied by a snuffling, grunting sound. The digging sounds grow louder and something sharp scrapes against the other side of the wall. The wall creaks and Tom feels the stones shudder against him. He tumbles backwards, just in time to avoid the wall as it collapses into a heap on the floor. Moonlight and fresh air stream in. Tom's dark-blind eyes are dazzled and he closes them tight.

When Tom looks up again he is astonished to see a pair of badgers watching him from a gap in the broken wall.

"What's he say?" asks Snout.

"Nothing," replies Brock. "He's just sitting there staring at me."

"Did you tell him we'd come to get him out?"

"He didn't seem to understand."

Snout pushes past Brock and peers down into the cellar.

"The sparrow said he was a cub, but he looks more like a full-grown."

"He smells alright, for a human," says Brock. "There's no harm in him."

"Why ain't he coming out?"

"His paws are tied. I'll go bite the binders off."

Brock clambers down the pile of earth and the boy shuffles back, giving off a strong fear scent.

"I'm here to help," growls Brock. "Stay still and I'll try and get your paws free."

The boy stops backing away. Brock noses gently towards the boy's tied paws and begins biting off the stuff wrapped around them. His teeth are sharp and the rope is soon shredded. The boy pulls his hands free and draws his lips back to show his teeth.

Brock scampers back, ready to fight, but Snout whispers down:

"They do that it when they're happy."

"Humans are strange creatures," replies Brock.

"Climb back out show him the way. He seems a bit slow on the uptake."

Brock scrambles up the pile of earth and turns to peer back into the cellar. The boy sits on the floor, staring at his hands in wonder.

"He's not that clever, is he?" says Snout.

Brock twitches his nose. He can hear the rattle of a carriage and smell humans and horses coming over the heath.

"Where's that bird gone?"

"He flew off," says Snout. "Said he had something else to do."

"We've done what he asked," says Brock. "I'm not hanging about. Them full-growns are coming back. They've got barking irons and they smell nasty."

"If he was a badger cub I'd pull him up with my teeth," mutters Snout.

"I don't think he'd like that."

"I expect he'll work it out eventually."

The badgers lumber away over the scrubby grass towards the trees. They are exposed out on the heath and eager to get back to the safety of their own territory.

They reach the edge of the wood and slip into the shadows.

Tom rubs his wrists and flexes his fingers. Did that really happen? Did a couple of badgers knock down the wall and bite the rope off him? Half dazed, he crawls up out of the hole.

He comes up beside a ramshackle cottage on the edge of a barren heath. There is a wood nearby and in the distance he can see a gallows silhouetted against the moon. There is no sign of the badgers.

Tom's sense of smell is not as good as Brock's but he soon hears the drumming of hooves and the clatter of wheels. He hears the carriage drawing to a halt on the far side of the cottage and creeps along the wall to get a closer look.

A two horse handsome cab is pulled up near the front door of the cottage. The cottage door opens and a man comes out with a lantern.

"That you Snudge?" he growls.

"Who else would it be?" says the coach driver.

"What about the others?"

"They're on their way."

Tom hears more hoofbeats and looks up to see a cart approaching. It draws up behind the carriage and the men sitting in the back jump out and come and stand in a group by the carriage door. There are eight of them in all and none of them look friendly. Tom recognises Charlie Angel and the other thieves from Hawkins Yard.

The door of the carriage opens and low voice speaks.

"Where's that chestnut mare? You was supposed to bring her along with you."

"Squire Colby took her," says a bald headed man with an eye patch."There was nothing we could do."

"When I give an order, I expect it to be carried out," hisses the man inside the carriage.

"Squire Colby's an uncanny gent," says Patch. "I'll tell you straight, he puts the Fear of God in me. We saw things down at Wytch Cross that ain't natural. That wolf of his -"

"Useless cully!" snaps the hidden man. He leans out of the shadows and Tom sees Mr Famish.

Famish sees the fear in his men's eyes. Charlie Angel is a cowardly little runt but it takes something big to scare cut-throats like Patch and Ned Bones. Famish's soul is hardened enough to be immune to all but the strongest enchantment but he is developing a grudging respect for Josia Colby's power. The deranged nonsense that Jimmy Twig was spouting last night is starting to make a little more sense.

Charlie Angel swallows hard and looks up at Famish:

"Mr Famish, Sir," he says. "Josia Colby said that he wants the rest of Ruby Gilbert's family; her father and her little sister. We're to bring them here and wait for his word."

"I won't take any more orders from Josia Colby until I see some of his gold," spits Famish. "I don't trust that fancy cove one inch." He shoots out a bony hand, grabs the front of Charlie Angel's coat and pulls the boy to him. He smiles and digs his fingernails into Charlie's cheek, drawing beads of blood. "If you want to keep you good looks then you'll go to Colby's house in Chelsea, find your way inside and take anything you can lay your hands on. Colby and his men are all busy down in Sussex tonight. it should be an easy enough job, even for a cockroach like you."

Charlie nods and Famish lets him go. He glares down the other men.

"After you've dropped Charlie off in Chelsea, the rest of you scum can earn your keep by heading over to Hawkins Yard. I want Ruby Gilbert's father and sister. Get them alive if you can but kill anyone who makes trouble. Take all the horses and burn the place to the ground."

"Colby just said to take the blind man and the girl," says Patch. "He didn't say anything about burning stuff down."

"You work for me, turd brain. I want to send out a message - no-one messes with Mr Famish." He spits on the ground at Patch's feet. "I gave you an order. Why are you still here?"

"The boys have been riding all night," says Patch, looking round at the other men for some back up. "We need a bit of shut-eye and some scran."

A couple of men nod in agreement but none of them raise their eyes to Mr Famish.

"There's grog in the house," says Mr Famish. "Sluice yer gobs and get on with it. The job needs doing tonight." He slams the carriage door and Snudge jumps up into the driving seat. The coach pulls away and the men fall back to the cottage, muttering under their breath.

A lantern flares behind the window and Tom peers past the ragged curtain to see Famish's men gathered around a fireplace, passing a bottle between them. They are busy for now but it won't be long before they are on their way again. The cart is Tom's best chance.

He'll have to turn it around quietly and make sure he gets a good way down the road before the gang come out if he's to have a hope of out-running them.

The horses are not keen to move. Tom whispers to them and pats them on the neck the way he's seen Ruby do but he does not have her touch. The horses ignore him and in the end he has to grab hold of their bridles and pull them. They dig in with their hooves but when Tom leans back and hauls on the straps they shuffle sullenly forward, one slow step at a time.

The cart is half way turned about when Tom hears a noise behind him.

Charlie Angel has not been invited inside to take a drink of rum with the other men. He has been left to watch the horses. This is Thornton Heath, after all, and the place is crawling with thieves. Charlie sits slumped in the shadows beside the front porch of the cottage, staring at his boots and feeling as sorry for himself as it is possible for a soul to be. Underneath the bravado and brash charm he is nothing but a lost boy, no more able to escape Mr Famish's clutches than Jimmy Twigg. Charlie has lived in terror of Mr Famish all his life but tonight he met someone who scares him more. Charlie saw Captain Ransome transform into a wolf, he saw Josia Colby change his face to become Tom, and he saw Patch Williams and the rest of Mr Famish's men submit to Josia Colby's will like lambs.

Charlie played the part that he was given. He sold Ruby Gilbert to Josia Colby and the rest of the Gilbert's will soon follow.

When you grow up in the gutter, the way Charlie did, betrayal comes as natural as breathing. So why does it bother him?

Charlie has never trusted anyone; he has never seen the use in it. He is stronger alone; thats how it's always been. But for a couple of days, as he and Tom and Ruby plotted the theft of the Faerie Star, Charlie caught a glimpse of what it might be like to have friends.

All that is gone now. Josia Colby will kill Ruby and, even if Tom lives to tell the tale, there's no way he will ever forgive Charlie.

Charlie is startled from his self pity by the sound of a snorting horse and looks up to see Tom standing by the cart.

How one earth did he get out of the cellar?

A shout is all it would take, and Patch and Ned would be out of the door, pulling Tom down.

Charlie says nothing. He crouches in the shadows, watching Tom as he turns the cart. Tom has his back to him and the flat bed of the cart is only a short sprint away. Charlie could jump up and hitch a ride without Tom even knowing. His life would be worth less than nothing in London if he ran away from Mr Famish but there are ships sailing from the docks every day. Perhaps it is time to start again? He could go to Spain or to the Americas. Anywhere would be better than here.

Charlie rolls to his feet and prepares to run but he stops dead at the sound of the cottage door opening.

Ned Bones sees what's happening at once.

"Oi!" he calls "Someone's after the horses!"
Ned pulls the pistol from his belt and points it at
Tom. Charlie sees Ned's thumb flick back the
hammer and his finger squeeze the trigger. Charlie is
up in a flash, knocking the gun out of Ned's hand.
They fall together as the pistol goes off, Ned's head
thuds into the door frame and the big man crumples
like a sack of potatoes. There are shouts and the
thunder of running boots from inside the cottage.
Charlie is on his feet in an instant. He pulls the door
shut, grabs up Ned's pistol and jams the barrel
through the rusty iron hoops that secure the padlock.

   The gun shot has spooked the horses and they are
eager to be away. They make the rest of the turn in
double quick time and Tom jumps up onto the
driving seat of the cart.
"Take me with you," shouts Charlie.
Tom darts Charlie a hate filled look and grabs up the
reins.
   The cottage door shudders under a heavy blow and
the hinges give way in a shower of rust and splinters.
Charlie runs. The horses are pulling away fast but he
throws himself forward in time to grab hold of the
back of the cart and haul himself aboard.
"Charlie's killed Ned!" roars Patch from the cottage
door. "I'll gizzard him."
Charlie turns in time to see the flash of powder from
Patch's rifle. The bullet punches into his chest and he
falls back onto the rough boards.
   Tom ducks low and urges the horses on. Their fear
of the guns gives them new strength and they are

soon pulling away at a stiff gallop. There are shouts of rage and a couple more shots but the sounds of pursuit soon fade.

The track from the cottage runs down past the gallows onto a well kept road. Tom pulls up and turns to look back into the bed of the cart. Charlie Angel lies there, pale and wide eyed. There is a dark stain on the front of his torn coat and blood is pooling on the boards around him.

"Are you dead?" asks Tom coldly.

"Not yet," croaks Charlie, opening his eyes.

"Which way to London?"

"Turn Right. The Turnpike runs straight up to Westminster."

"I should leave you on the road," says Tom."But you saved my life back there."

"They shot me," says Charlie.

"No more than you deserve," growls Tom.

"I'm sorry," says Charlie. "I'm sorry I sold you out to Mr Famish. You don't know what he's like."

"Save your breath," mutters Tom, turning away. " It looks as if you've precious little left to waste."

He calls to the horses and they gallop on up the road back to London.

Chapter 23 - The Widow's Well

Ruby's hands have been tied in front and her legs
have been lashed to Dervish's girth straps. Her pistols
are gone, the leather belt slung over Mr Furey's
shoulder. There is nothing she can do but let Josia
Coby lead her where he will. Mr Furey follows
behind, pulling the huge grey wolf on a chain.
Dervish is too exhausted to run from the beast any
longer and she simply plods on with her head down,
giving an occasional shiver of fear.

Ruby rests her face against the warmth of Dervish's
neck. She is truly beaten. The Kern and the Faerie
Star are gone and she has no hope of any help. She
has no idea what Josia Colby wants from her. He
means to kill her, she is certain of that. She can only
pray that her death will be swift.

The horses halt and Ruby lifts her head. They are at
the edge of a small clearing.
"Tie the beasts up," orders Josia Colby.
Mr Furey winds the wolf's iron chain around a tree
and ties Dervish and the white stallion to another on
the far side of the clearing. He gives a vicious tug on
the rope tied around Ruby's left leg and the sudden
pain makes her gasp.
"You don't know what pain is," says Mr Furey. "But
by the time we are through with you -"
"Be quiet," hisses Josia Colby. "Keep your eyes on
Ransome. I don't want him getting free."
Josia Colby strides to the middle of the glade. The
moon is setting behind the trees, leaving only the

sparks of the stars to illuminate the night. The Squire takes a book from his pocket and Ruby recognises The Keys of Queen Mab. How long is it since she took the book from Mr Periwigge on Reaver's Hill? Half a year ago? It seems a lifetime.

Josia Colby begins to chant, his voice ringing loud in the silence of the wood:

"Calathon alata'bey darkesta,
Calata celesta cassaita -"

The edges of the world begin to blur. Faint with pain and exhaustion, Ruby slips into a trance. The air in the clearing shimmers and a wind rises, shivering the winter branches. The darkness deepens and Ruby looks up to see the stars falling from the sky.

It is only when a cold flake lands on Ruby's cheek that she understands that it is snow falling. She squints up to see ragged clouds rushing overhead, blotting out the last of the stars.

Squire Colby stands with the open book in his hand, snow swirling about him.

"I have summoned you," he commands. "Reveal yourself."

A slim shadow slips from the trees and stalks forward into the clearing.

"What do you wish?" asks a soft voice.

Ruby sees a man dressed in a blue coat lined with silver fur. He wears black riding boots and his dark hair curls down to his collar. His skin is as pale as ice and his eyes are an unfathomable colour. It is Perian, Queen Mab's messenger.

Perian sweeps the glade with his gaze, taking in Josia Colby, Mr Furey and the grey wolf. He looks over at the horses and flashes a grin at Ruby. The faerie steps nearer to Josia Colby, the snow swirling at his back. A host of figures appear in the whirling whiteness; eagles, wolves, sabre toothed cats and great bears, stags with antlers of ice and wild eyed women with windblown silver hair. A howling song comes from the lips of the ice women and they lean out over Perian's shoulders, their snowy fingers reaching for Josia Colby.

For a moment the snow spirits seemed poised to engulf Squire Colby but he mutters a word, gives a wave of his hand, and the shapes dissolve back into swirling snow. The wind gusts up and sweeps the snow flurry away into the trees.

"Enough tricks," says Josia Colby, his eyes sharp with annoyance. "Kneel before me."

Perian goes down on one knee in front of Josia Colby but there is no hint of subservience in his eyes.

"You have spoken the words of command," says Perian. "But there is pact to be made if you seek my aid."

"Serve me and I will let you live," says Josia Colby coldly. "That is the only pact I shall make. I may have need of a messenger when I sit upon Queen Mab's throne."

Perian laughs, and the sound of it fills Ruby's heart with sudden hope; here is someone who has no fear of Josia Colby.

Perian looks at the book in Squire Colby's hands:

"You would not be the first sorcerer to mistake that book of rhymes for true power -"

"Silence!" hisses Josia Colby. He reaches into his coat and takes out the Faerie Star. He holds the diamond up, shimmering with stolen starlight, and the smile fades from Perian's face. "I hold the heart of Queen Mab's magic in my hand," says Josia Colby." I have learned the words of unmaking and, when the time comes, I will cast Queen Mab down."

"You are a fool," whispers Perian." No mortal could ever rule the Twilight Land."

"I shall rule it or I shall lay it waste," says Josia Colby. "I do not care which." He fixes Perian with his grey eyes and begins to chant a new spell:

"Khelthra to'ahchen, khlethra chalaran-"

Perian's face contorts in pain and he falls forward, gasping for breath.

"Would you like me to finish reciting that particular rhyme?" asks Josia Colby.

Perian shakes his head.

"Even the immortal Sidhe can be mastered," says Josia Colby, his eyes bright with triumph. "You will do as I command."

Perian nods, his expression stony.

"I seek the Widow's Well, near the Long Man's Gate. It is a crossing place," says Josia Colby. "Do you know it?"

"It is an accursed place," says Perian.

"I did not ask your opinion. I ask only that you guide us there. "

"It is not far, by Faerie reckoning," says Perian." If you were to take hold of my hand then the two of us might fly there in a moment, walking upon the air." He shrugs and looks around the glade. "But to transport the whole company is beyond my art. I fear that we must walk."

"How near is it?" asks Squire Colby.

"That depends upon the path that we take."

"Do not trifle with me. Take us to the Widow's Well by the most direct way. We must be there before the night is done."

"As you command."

Perian jumps to his feet and steps away into the trees. Josia Colby unties the horses, mounts up on the white stallion and pulls Ruby and Dervish after him.

Snow falls from the branches as they push through the trees, dusting their faces with ice. The trees grow thick and close and Ruby and Squire Colby have to lean low in their saddles to duck under the boughs. The horses snort with annoyance at the scratching branches and Mr Furey curses at the brambles. They push on, skidding down a slippery bank into a frozen bog. Grey ice splinters under the horses hooves and they sink down into the foul water. The horses trudge on as Perian skips nimbly ahead, his feet quite dry, using fallen tree trunks as stepping stones. Mr Furey scowls and wades knee deep into the ice cold filth but the wolf halts at the edge of the bog and refuses to go in. It hauls back on its chain and Mr Furey is pulled over onto his back, splashing and cursing.

"This is no time to sleep, Mr Furey," says Perian. "We must keep up a good pace if we are to reach the Widow's Well by dawn."

Mr Furey gives Perian a murderous look and yanks hard on the wolf's chain.

"Move it, you filthy beast!" he growls. "I'm wet through. No reason why you should stay dry."

The wolf stands its ground, raising its hackles and snarling, until Squire Colby stops to mutter a word of command. The great beast drops its head like beaten dog and slinks forward into the freezing mire.

They splash and stumble through the ice and mud and climb out to clamber up the side of a rocky hill. Perian ignores the wide path running along the top of the hill and disappears into the thorny undergrowth on the far side.

"If you are leading us astray then you will suffer for it," says Josia Colby.

"We are travelling true as an arrow," calls Perian from deep in the trees. "Directly to the place that you commanded."

Josia Colby scowls at the impenetrable thicket ahead of them.

"Come here, sprite."

Perian re-appears, stepping through the branches without a single thorn scratch.

"Yes, Master?"

"You know full well that we cannot pass through here."

Perian appears baffled. He points away through the trees:

"I do as you command, Master. You wished me to take you by the most direct way and I am doing so, as straight as a crow flies."

"Do not mock me," says Josia Colby, his eyes cold with rage. "I command you to lead us to the Widow's Well by as swift a way as you can contrive but it shall be along pathways fit for the passage of men and horses."

"Of course," says Perian. He bows turns away along the path, giving Ruby a mischievous wink as he goes. "May I ask what you seek at The Widows Well?" he calls back over his shoulder. "They say that a battle was fought upon that land, long ago, and that the victors burned the bodies of their fallen enemies and threw their charred bones into the well. They say that spirits of the dead warriors linger there and any who drinks from the poisoned water can speak with them. Do you seek council from the dead, Squire Colby? It is a common error among sorcerers; to imagine that unquiet souls have anything of use to say. I generally find the dead peevish and dull and quite devoid of interesting conversation."

"My reasons are my own," growls Josia Colby."Speak no more until I command it."

Perian nods his head and falls silent, but a moment later he begins to sing, loud and high, his voice a perfect mimicry of a London street urchin:

"In the city of Westminster
There lived a rat catcher's daughter
Her father caught rats and she sold sprats
All around the -"

"Be quiet," says Squire Colby.

Ruby has to bite her lip to stop herself from laughing.

"I am yours to command," says Perian brightly. "But if I fail you then it is no fault of my own. I am compelled by our pact to take you at your word, that is the nature of the spell."

"If you speak again, unasked, then I shall tell Mr Furey to let the wolf tear your throat out. I imagine even a faerie might die of such a wound?"

"I might die of it," says Perian thoughtfully. "But then you would never reach your destination."

"I command you to lead us directly, by good paths, to the Widow's Well," hisses Josia Colby through gritted teeth. "And you will not speak or sing or chant as we go. That is all."

Perian nods his head and steps away along the path. A moment later he begins to whistle, a sound so tuneless, shrill and awful that the horses snort and the wolf begins to howl.

"Be utterly silent!" roars Josia Colby. "Not a single noise from you."

The whistling stops and Perian leads them on in dignified silence. He steps into a pool of shadow and is gone. In his place is a fox, large as a dog and lithe as a cat. The creature turns to look back at them, its shifting eyes glinting with mischief. It gives a shrug and trots on ahead.

Perian's insolence waters the tiny seed of hope in Ruby's heart. She leans forward to rest on Dervish's neck. She is cold down to the marrow of her bones and the awful pain in her leg is sapping her strength.

Even so, the slow rocking of the horse's walk lulls her, at last, into a fitful sleep. High above, the wind sweeps the snow clouds away and the stars flare up once more over the frost dusted land.

Ruby is woken by another jolt of pain. She opens her eyes to see Mr Furey standing with his hand on her injured leg, grinning nastily.

"We have come to your final resting place," he says. "Take your last look at the world."

They stand in a circle of twisted trees, at the centre of which rises a stone well, half buried beneath a tangle of briars and blackthorn. A freezing mist rises from the well, bringing the stink of damp and death.

Perian sits a little way off, still in fox shape, watched over by the wolf. Josia Colby's horse is tied to one of the twisted trees and its master is standing by the briar choked well.

Squire Colby raises a hand and the thorn bushes surrounding the well catch fire. In the flare of flame Ruby sees that the encircling trees are dead and rotten. Beyond them is a high hedge of thorns.

The fire dies down and the scrubby trees about the well fall to ashes. Josia Colby turns to Ruby.

"Your trials are almost over, Ruby Gilbert, " he says. The expression on his face is one of tender cruelty. "You are a brave soul and a worthy sacrifice. Your death will open the gate for my allies to enter this world."

"Only a fool would summons ghosts to aid him," says Perian.

"I bound you to silence," hisses Josia Colby.

"I have fulfilled our pact by leading you here," says the fox with a smile. "If you wish to bind me once more then you must speak the rhyme. Until then, I am free to choose my own destiny." The fox swishes its tail and crouches back on its haunches. "I choose to thwart you, Squire Colby. You shall not take Ruby Gilbert's life. "

The fox leaps and as it flies through the air it seems to grow larger. Squire Colby puts up his hands to protect his face from the sharp white teeth and stumbles back against the fire blackened rim of the well. The fox sinks its teeth into Squire Colby's hand and rakes at his face with its claws. Roaring with rage, Josia Colby topples back. He seems poised to fall into the well's mouth but at the last moment he reaches out a hand to steady himself. His right hand finds the fox's throat and he throws the snarling beast off.

The fox rolls into a crouch, ready to spring again, but Perian has forgotten about Mr Furey. The rat faced man throws himself onto the fox, wrapping the iron wolf chain around the its neck and pulling it tight. The fox gives a yelp of pain and falls to the ground, twisting and clawing at the rusty iron. "Serve you right, vermin scum," hisses Mr Furey as he winds the chain tighter around the fox's body. He looks hopefully up at Squire Colby. "Shall I drown it?"

"Do not kill him yet," mutters the Squire."The sprite may still be of use." He wraps a handkerchief around his bloody hand and kneels down on the ground beside the bound fox. He smiles as the creature shrinks back from him in terror. "It seems that the old tales about iron having power over the Faerie race is true. I shall have to find suitable chains for Queen Mab." Josia Colby laughs and gives a tug on the end of the chain. "I shall deal with you in good time, sprite. Until then, I command you to remain your animal shape and to stir neither limb nor tongue until I ask it."

Ruby's heart goes cold at the sight of Perian so tightly bound. He looks so small and helpless, wrapped in the cruel iron chain, but as the Squire turns away, the fox looks up at Ruby and winks. Perian cannot move his body but his eyes dance about, flicking up to Ruby's face, over to the trees and back again.

When she is certain that none of the men are watching, Ruby turns to look into the branches. She sees a small shape fluttering there. She glances back at Perian and he winks.

Squire Colby takes a bundle of cloth from his saddle bag and rolls it out on the scorched earth at the foot of the well. Ruby turns again to look for the sparrow but it is gone. On a nearby branch another shape moves. Tiny and brown, the mouse comes creeping to the end of the branch. It stands up on its haunches, twitching its whiskers, gazing up at Ruby with shiny black eyes. The little creature gathers itself and makes a great leap, flying through the air to land on the edge of Dervish's saddle. Claws scrabbling on the smooth leather, it scampers up onto Ruby's arm and runs down to the rope at her wrists.

The mouse sets to work at once, nibbling the strands of rope with its tiny teeth. Ruby watches in amazement as more mice leap from the branch and come skittering over the saddle to bite at the ropes binding her. She sits as still as she can, not daring to lift her eyes, hoping against hope that the mice will go unnoticed.

Ruby feels the ropes loosen at her wrists and ankles. She shakes her hands free but leaves the rope draped over them, just in case. The mice turn and scamper away, leaping back off the edge of the saddle onto the branch. Ruby glances up at Perian and his fox eyes twinkle back.

"Just a moment longer," Perian's voice whispers in her ear. How he speaks to her she cannot guess, for the fox's lips remain closed.

Josia Colby has set five black candles into silver holders and stood them around the rim of the well. In the centre of the black cloth lies a tarnished iron bowl and steel knife with a curved blade. The book lies open in Josia Colby's hand and he is bent over it, intent upon the words of the incantation.

Ruby's broken ankle throbs with a fresh wave of pain. She lets the pain wash through her and out the other side, she lets the force of it sing in her nerves and bones. She is wide awake and ready for anything. Dervish senses the change in Ruby and trembles with anticipation. Ruby flexes her aching fingers and prepares to ride.

There is a sound like wind in the leaves. The noise grows louder, becoming a rushing whirr, and the night is torn open by a great shrieking. Josia Colby looks up in astonishment to see a cloud of screaming darkness plummeting down from the sky.

Rooks, ravens, blackbirds and crows, hawks, owls, magpies and gulls; more birds than can be counted - falling in a swarm of slashing beaks and razor claws, their wings blotting out the stars.

The initial assault is so fierce and unexpected that Josia Colby and Mr Furey are driven to their knees, their hands clamped over their faces to protect their eyes. They clamber up, screaming to each other, running blindly, desperate to shake off their attackers. Mr Furey runs into a tree and is knocked flat on his back, while the grey wolf snaps and snarls. A hawk swoops down, shrieking and taunting the maddened wolf and it leaps up after it, jaws snapping shut on empty air. The leap takes the grey wolf to the edge of the well. It puts its paws up on the rim and when the hawk swoops again it jumps higher. The Hawk slides away into the night and the grey wolf falls, howling, into the well.

The birds flow past Ruby and Dervish, ignoring them completely. They ignore the Squire's stallion but the horse is terrified by the commotion and it rears up, tossing its head and pulling at its tether. The branch snaps and the horse leaps away into the night. Dervish snorts and shuffles back but she does not bolt.

"Now!" says Perian's voice in Ruby's ear.

Ruby peers through the mist of birds at the little fox, still bound tight in its chains. She cannot leave him. She urges Dervish forward, determined to take Perian with her.

"Have no fear for me," whispers Perian's voice. *"Run! The birds will not hold Squire Colby back for long."*

Josia Colby has already shaken off most of his attackers. He has one hand over his eyes and his lips are moving. A moment later the black candles at the edge of the well burst into life. The flames swirl up into a whirling funnel of flame and the birds scatter like a whirlwind.

Dervish leaps away. The hedge beyond the circle of trees is thick and high. There must be a gate somewhere but Ruby has no idea where it might be. She is turning about to spy an escape when she feels a gust of wind on her cheek. A bird darts down past her into the thorn trees and she stares in wonder as the branches creak and twist apart. A tunnel appears, its walls woven from curling branches. At the far end a sparrow is winging its way out into the sky.

Dervish gallops into the gap. The branches quiver as they pass and swish back behind them, leaving an impassible thicket.

A scatter of stars, the thunder of hooves, and the night takes them.

Chapter 24 - The Long Man's Gate

Ruby opens her eyes to see a patch of starry sky. She is in a dark place. She can smell earth, rotting wood and leaf-mould and she feels strangely warm, despite the cold of the night. She sits up to find herself lying on a drift of leaves inside the hollow of a great grandfather oak. Dervish stands nearby, watching her calmly from beneath the great tree's shadow. Ruby has the distinct feeling that someone else was here with them, only a moment before, but they are gone now.

She remembers the headlong flight from the Widow's Well and the fall from the saddle. Then what?

Dervish comes forward and puts her head down to nuzzle at a ragged bundle of feathers lying on the leaves at Ruby's side. Ruby lifts the sparrow in her hands but it lies limp, wings loose, head lolling.
"No!" she gasps. "You can't be dead."
She strokes the sparrow's head but the eyes do not open.

Ruby's eyes fill with tears. The brave bird must have given the last of its strength in rescuing her. Ever since that fateful day in Bascome when Ruby saved it from the clutches of the shadow hawk, the sparrow has watched over her. It came to her in her prison cell and it led her to the Faerie Star. The sight of the little thing lying broken in her hand is almost too much to bear.
"Brave Ragwort," whispers Ruby through her tears." I hope that I can be worthy of your sacrifice."

184

Did Squire Colby find a way to open the gate at the well? And what of Perian? How much time has passed while she lay under the oak?

Ruby knows that she has no choice but to go after Josia Colby once more. It might be hopeless but there is too much at stake to turn back now. Ragwort gave everything; so must she.

Ruby folds the sparrow's wings and gently slips the bird into the breast pocket of her jacket.

A scream shatters the quiet of the night - an awful, despairing sound, cut off almost as soon as it begins, leaving a chilly silence in its wake. Dervish gives a snort of fear and stamps at the earth. Ruby gets to her feet and puts a hand on the chestnut mare's neck. It is only as she climbs up onto Dervish's back that she realises that the pain in her ankle has lessened. Her leg still twinges when she puts her weight on it but the ankle seems to be healing remarkably fast. Was this Ragwort's last gift?

There is no time to wonder about this small miracle. Ruby nudges Dervish forward and they ride out from under the oak and away into the wood, heading in the direction of the deathly scream.

They find a path and after half a mile or so they come to the thorny hedge around the Widow's Well. The path runs on under an arch of woven branches but Dervish refuses to enter. Ruby leaves Dervish at the gate and limps on alone.

The grove is utterly silent. The whole place stinks of burning and there are broken feathers scattered everywhere. There are no fallen birds but the ground is marked by the passage of many feet.

The candlesticks still stand on the rim of the well and the iron bowl lies on its side in the mud, glistening wetly. Beside the well lies a huddled figure. The man's face is turned away from Ruby but from the bandage on his hand and the pistol belt flung over his shoulder she knows that it must be Mr Furey.

She limps forward to kneel on the ground beside him. He lies quite still and when she tugs the belt of pistols out from under his arm he does not stir. She is glad that she cannot see his face.

"No-one deserves to die that way," she whispers. "Not even Mr Furey."

It could so easily have been her.

The way that she must take is clear enough; a ragged hole has been burned into the hedge and a path trodden through the gap. She cannot tell how many were in the company; ten or twenty? Certainly more than she could ever hope to fight. She checks and loads her pistols and limps back to Dervish.

Dervish does not like the path but she suffers it for Ruby's sake. It runs through fields and woods, straight as an arrow, from the Widow's Well toward a ridge of hills a couple of miles ahead. Everything lying across the path has been burned to ash; trees, bushes, hedges and fences. If it weren't for the bootprints in the mud, Ruby might guess the track had been made by a dragon.

The path cuts over a lane and Ruby sees the charred remains of a signpost lying in the hedge: Alfriston,

Wilmington, Mickelham, Newhaven. On the far side of the lane the burned path runs into a wood where the stumps of fallen trees hiss and smoulder.

Ruby nudges Dervish on into a slow walk, eyes and ears alert for danger. What manner of allies has Squire Colby summoned from the well? Ghosts or demons?

At the far side of the wood, the burned path runs out into an open field. Ruby looks up and gasps; looming above them is the bone pale outline of a giant a hundred feet high. Eyeless and faceless, with a tall staff in each outstretched hand, he stands as still as the dark hills behind him.

Ruby sees the truth; the figure has been cut into the turf, leaving white chalk lines against the dark earth. "The Long Man's Gate," whispers Ruby.
In a clearing at the chalk giant's feet stand a group of dark robed figures. Ruby counts twelve of them. Their faces are pale and they carry swords in their hands. A spark of red flame illuminates the face of Josia Colby, kneeling on the ground beside them.

Ruby leads Dervish back into the trees.
"I'll not tie you up," she says, stroking the mare's neck. "You've been brave to come so far with me and I shan't ask you to go any further." The chestnut mare nuzzles into Ruby's shoulder. "Wait for me, if you can."

Ruby limps slowly on over the frozen field, keeping as far from the burned path as she can. She makes for the trees at the foot of the hill and creeps along the edge of the wood toward the gathered figures.

"Be swift," says Torment. "The Lychway is already fading. The snivelling soul that you offered in sacrifice did not have much life in him."

Torment and the other furies seem solid enough but when Josia Colby turns to look at them he sees the stars glimmering through their pale skin. He turns back to the hill, raises the Kern in one hand and the Faerie Star in the other.

"With Wayland Smith's key, I open the gate," he calls. "With Loki's diamond, I summon you, Queen Mab. Step into the Waking World!"

The darkness deepens at the chalk giant's feet. An archway appears and at the heart of the darkness a tall figure appears. Queen Mab is even more beautiful than Ruby remembers. Dark haired and pale skinned, she wears a coat of white fur and crown of mistletoe. Her eyes catch and magnify the starlight and a soft glow flows from her, animating everything that it touches. Green shoots come curl up from the frozen ground at her feet and white snowdrops unfurl.

Behind Queen Mab are a host of faerie knights, dressed in silver mail and furred cloaks, holding spears and bows. There are musicians too, with harps and drums and silver pipes.

Among the musicians stands Davey.

Ruby's heart leaps at the sight of him. He has the same dreaming look upon his face that he wore when Queen Mab first took him away, but it is him.

Queen Mab halts before the dark robed figures. She looks down at the chained fox at Josia Colby's feet and her eyes glitter with rage. She looks up at the

Furies and her rage becomes a cold fire. Her voice is ice and steel.

"Twice you have betrayed me," she says to the Furies.

"Be silent," says Josia Colby."Kneel before your summoner."

Queen Mab turns the storm of her rage upon Josia Colby and fear flickers in his eyes.

"The Gods bow down to me," says Queen Mab."I kneel to no-one."

"I hold the heart of all your magic," says Josia Colby, holding up the Faerie Star in a shaking hand. "I can unmake you, if I wish to."

"Foolish mortal -"

"Asht'eck orphano sheoth," chants Josia Colby. The diamond pulses with sharp green light and Queen Mab falls to her knees.

"This cannot be - "

"Sheoth Khal'em ophio -"

The diamond flares brighter, while the light coming from Queen Mab seems to dim. The leaves wither in her hair and the youth fades from her cheeks. She begins to age.

"You will submit to me," says Josia Colby

Queen Mab's cloak is cobweb grey and her hair is silver, but she is still beautiful and her eyes are the same - fierce and bright.

"Never!"

"You will submit or you will be turned to dust."

Ruby cannot stand by and let this happen. Queen Mab stole Davey from the waking world. She is capricious and selfish, proud and cruel, but her cruelty is the cruelty of the wild wood, the cruelty of the storm and of winter. She is a force of nature, a part of the balance of the world. What might happen if she were to perish? Ruby has no way of knowing, but one thing is certain; if Josia Colby gains even a portion of Queen Mab's power then there will be no end to the evil he will work.

Ruby takes hold of her pistol and steps out from the cover of the trees. One of the dark robed figures gives a cry, raises her sword and leaps forward. Torment is moving fast but Ruby still has time. She takes aim. "Turn and face me!" she calls. "Or I will shoot you in the back."

Josia Colby turns:

"This one is no danger to us," he says to Torment.

"No mortal weapon can harm me now."

Ruby pulls the trigger and a white hot spark flashes in the air before Josia Colby's heart. An aura of blue flame flares up around him and the bullet falls harmlessly to the grass. Josia Colby smiles, lifts his hand and Ruby is bound tight by his enchantment.

She falls to her knees, all hope gone.

Torment steps back to Josia Colby's side and smiles down at Queen Mab, kneeling on the ground, white haired and frail.

"Even the immortals shall die," says Josia Colby. He raises the diamond one again but before he can shape the last words a leaping blur of silver comes rushing from the trees. The silver wolf knocks Josia Colby off his feet, spilling the diamond and the spell book onto the ground.

The battle cry of the Furies tears open the night, savage and unearthly, full of spite and rage. They surge forward, driving the wolf back and encircling it. The beast turns about in the tightening ring of steel, snarling and snapping at the sword blades. "Kill her!" commands Josia Colby, pulling himself up again. His face is bloody and his left arm hangs limp at his side.

Torment steps into the circle of Furies and raises her blade to strike at the silver wolf.

Queen Mab is on her feet, her white hair flowing out behind her, striding forward to grab up the diamond. But Josia Colby reaches out his good arm and speaks a single word and the Faerie Star flies to his hand. He holds up the diamond and turns to meet the Faerie Queen.

"Orpen'ec ashk'e -"

The protective aura of blue light still flickers around Josia Colby but the silver wolf's attack has broken the binding charm that held Ruby. She feels the spell losen its grip and she reaches for her pistol.

"Khal'ck sharak," calls Josia Colby.

Queen Mab stands rooted to the spot, her eyes wide with terror. She falls to her knees, her fingers withering like old twigs.

Ruby aims and pulls the trigger. It is a desperate shot and a hopeless chance but it is all that she can do.

The bullet flies true, straight into the heart of the Faerie Star. The diamond explodes in a crash of summer lightning, scattering sparks and stars of light. The stars fly into Queen Mab, they fly into

Josia Colby, they fly into the chained fox and into the Furies. Light sparks fly into the crouching silver wolf and into Ruby. Ruby's eyes are so filled with light that she cannot see. Her ears and mouth are full of light, her brain, her belly, her bones and her breath are made of light. There is a great rush of wind, a wave of song and a gust of wild laughter. The earth trembles and roars and Ruby tastes rain and spring leaves, she tastes honey and ice, sunlight and darkness. There is a cry of despair and a rolling clap of thunder.

The night returns, cold and clear. Ruby is kneeling on the hard earth with the pistol in her hand. She looks up.

Queen Mab stands over Josia Colby, who has slumped down to his knees, his head bowed. Perian stands at Queen Mab's side, in human shape once more. He turns to Ruby and winks.

Queen Mab is young again, her eyes are clear and her body is unbent. Her hair is raven black and her robe is as blue as starlight. The light around her seems brighter than ever.

There is no sign of the Furies and in the place where the silver wolf stood there crouches a pale girl. One of Queen Mab's knights steps forward, takes off his cloak and wraps it around her. The girl gets to her feet and Ruby recognises Lucy Cotton.

Perian picks up the fallen book and hands it to Queen Mab. A word from her and the book bursts into flame, the ashes swirl into darting shadows and a cloud of moths scatter to the four winds.

Queen Mab turns her gaze upon Josia Colby.

"Look at me," she commands.

The Squire raises his head.

"Let us see your true face," says the Faerie Queen. The man before her withers. His hair whitens and falls, his skin dries like old leaves and his body sags. He becomes a half dead thing, little more than a skeleton held together with twisted strips of flesh. His eyes sink back into the sockets of his skull but they do not close. They stare up at the Faerie Queen in terror and hatred.

"You sought immortality," says Queen Mab. "Perhaps I should bestow it upon you?" She laughs. "I curse you, Nathaniel Colby, to remain alive, trapped in the ruin of your body. You shall know the pains of age and the ache of hunger but no food or drink may pass your lips. No magic may aid you, nor any human kindness. I curse you to wander the Nine Worlds unceasing, until the end of time, as a reminder of what befalls any who are foolish enough to bring harm to me."

The withered man gets haltingly to his feet, like a puppet pulled by invisible strings.

"Only one thing may bring you release," says Queen Mab. "Only if one of those who you have wronged were to forgive you for the harm that you have done may you die. Only if you are truly forgiven may you go into Queen Morven's land."

There ancient man's eyes glitter with mad spite. His lips curl back over his toothless gums and he leans forward to spit on the ground at Mab's feet. No spittle comes. Instead, he doubles up, coughing and wheezing, his body wracked with pain. He falls to his knees, gasping for breath.

Ruby watches her enemy as he crawls away from Queen Mab. She feels no fear of him but the insane light in his eyes is horrible to see. Why does Queen Mab not destroy him? The Faerie Queen's pride is her greatest weakness; just as she could not believe that a mortal could ever become strong enough to challenge her, she cannot see the harm that she might do in letting what remains of Squire Colby go free. He is as weak as a kitten but he still has a tongue in his head and a voice to spill poison into unsuspecting ears.

This is the man who murdered Ruby's mother. He tore up their peaceful life in Bascome Valley and blighted the lives of so many others. He rewarded Mr Furey's loyalty with callous murder and summoned the Furies from the widow's well. He deserves the punishment that Mab has laid upon him but Ruby knows that she cannot let him slink away into the night. The world must be rid of him.

"I forgive him," says Ruby.

Squire Colby halts in his stumbling progress and stares up at her, unbelieving.

"No!" he hisses. "I do not want it."

"You have wronged me more times than I can count," says Ruby. "I cannot forgive all of the evil you have worked - the countless others who have died at your hands, or been enslaved by you, the others whose lives you have ruined. But I forgive the portion of pain that you have inflicted upon me."

"Are you certain?" asks Queen Mab.

Ruby looks into the Squire's eyes. She sees his rage and his despair, his agony and fear. His power gone, he is simply human. He came into the world a helpless, trusting creature and the world bent him into a twisted shape. It is time for that shape to dissolve. Once he is gone, the pain that he has inflicted can begin to heal.

"I forgive," says Ruby. "Let the world be free of him. There is enough fear and suffering here already. We do not need reminding of it."

Queen Mab bows her head to Ruby in a gesture of respect.

"I undo the curse," says Queen Mab. "Mortal born, from dust you come, to dust you go."

The Squire's body crumbles, his empty clothes fall, and a gust of wind scatters his ashes upon the air.

Chapter 25 - The Three Keys

Ruby looks over at Davey, standing among Queen Mab's courtiers. He is enchanted still and he makes no sign of having seen her. With a shiver of dread, Ruby realises that this might be the last time she ever sees him. She promised to return the Faerie Star to Queen Mab but, instead, she has destroyed it.

"What becomes of our bargain now?" she says. "What happens to Davey?"

Queen Mab is silent for a moment, her eyes fixed upon the sky.

"You are very like your ancestor, Wayland Smith," says the Faerie Queen. "Your soul is bright, like his, and you are brave and true." She turns her eyes to Ruby. "When you destroyed the Faerie Star you did me a much greater service than you could ever know. I see now how Loki wove his spells about the diamond. I was beguiled by the beauty of the jewel and believed that it increased my power but, all the while, it was drawing magic from me. The magic is returned to its proper place now and the debt that I owe you is great, Ruby Gilbert. I could bestow untold wealth upon you or work great wonders in your name."

"All I want is for Davey to be returned to the Waking World."

"Davey Tachard has dwelt in the Twilight Land. He has drunk Fairie wine and eaten our food." Queen Mab smiles sadly. "He cannot return. Even I cannot change his fate."

"You made a promise," says Ruby. "You told me that you would set him free."

"You may be re-united with him whenever you wish," says Queen Mab. She opens her hand to show Ruby the Kern. The battered old charm is remade. The lines are clear and bright and a green jewel flashes in the galloping horse's eye. Queen Mab crosses the distance between them and places the Kern into Ruby's hand. "This key is yours, by birth, and with it you may pass into my realm whenever you wish. Davey will always be here."

"That's not what I meant, and you know it. You lied to me!" says Ruby. "You are no better than Loki, nothing but a trickster!"

Queen Mab's eyes flicker with rage.

"Be careful, mortal. I am not minded to grant favours to those who scorn me."

"Your majesty," says Perian softly, stepping to the Faerie Queen's side. "I believe that there may be a way to grant Ruby Gilbert's wish. Wayland Smith made three keys, did he not? Ruby Gilbert holds the horse charm known as the Kern."

"What of it?" says Queen Mab. "The others were lost long ago."

"Not lost, exactly," says Perian with a grin. He reaches into the pocket of his blue coat and takes out a pair of golden pendants. They are like the Kern but depict a stooping hawk and running hare. Ruby remembers the fateful night on Reaver's hill when she first laid eyes on the book of faerie magic; a horse, a hawk and a hare engraved in gold upon the cover.

'How did you come by these?" asks Queen Mab, taking the charms from Perian.

"They are from the treasure hoard of a demon king," says Perian with a shrug. "How I acquired them is a long story, Your Majesty."

"You are right," says Queen Mab. "I see how it might be done." She laughs, her anger at Ruby gone as soon as it came. She turns to beckon Davey forward from the shadow of the gateway and he comes to kneel at her feet.

"Davey Tachard," says Queen Mab. "You are forever bound to the Twilight Land." She lifts the hawk charm and Ruby sees that the hawk's eye is a clear blue sapphire. "But, so long as you wear this key about your neck, you may pass the gates of Faerie as you please. If you wish to remain in the Waking World with Ruby Gilbert then you are free to do so, on one condition; that you return to my palace at the turn of each new moon, as all my servants must, and tell me all that you have seen in the lands of mortals." Queen Mab puts the hawk charm about Davey's neck. He blinks, rubs his eyes and shudders. He looks up at Queen Mab and turns to Ruby.

"Ruby?" he says. "Is that really you?" The dreamy expression has gone and his eyes are bright.

"It is."

He grins and reaches for her hand.

"You came back for me."

"Of course."

Ruby throws her arms about Davey's neck and he hugs her back, neither one wishing to let the other go.

Queen Mab turns to Lucy Cotton, wrapped in a cloak the colour of leaf shadows.

"Without your courage I would have been unmade," says Queen Mab. "How may I reward you, Lucy Cotton? Shall I find you a Faerie prince to marry? Shall I give you magic, wealth or fame?"

Lucy turns red and looks at her feet.

"Your Majesty, there is one thing." She looks up at Queen Mab. "Squire Colby laid a curse on me. Every night I change shape and become a wolf. Might you have the power to undo it?"

"The sorcerer's spells died with him," says Mab. "The curse is already broken." She looks hard at Lucy. "But magic like that leaves its mark. Your bones have become used to changing and it would be a shame to let such a talent go to waste." Queen Mab takes a silver ring from her finger and holds it out to Lucy. "If you ever wish to change your shape then all you must do is put on this ring and wish for it. You may take any form you choose, human or animal. You may run like wolf or fly like an eagle, you may swim like an otter or take the likeness of the Queen of Sweden." Queen Mab laughs. "Use the power as you wish."

Lucy closes her fingers over the ring and curtsies to Queen Mab.

"Thank you, Your Majesty."

"I also give you Wayland Smith's third key." Queen Mab takes the hare charm and puts it around Lucy's neck. "You and your descendants are free to travel into my realm whenever you wish - whatever shape they might take."

Queen Mab turns back to Ruby.

"There is one more who must be honoured," she says. "Ruby Gilbert, bring me the fallen sparrow."

Ruby takes the bundle of feathers from her jacket and hands it gently to Queen Mab. The Faerie Queen lifts the fallen bird to her lips and blows onto it.

"Brave Ragwort, awake! Come back with us into the Blessed Land."

The sparrow shivers and sits up on Queen Mab's palm. It opens its eyes and shakes its wings. With a joyful chirrup the bird takes to the air, bobbing up and circling twice around Ruby's head before darting away toward the Faerie Gate.

"Ruby Gilbert and Lucy Cotton," says Queen Mab. "I shall not forget what you have done for me. You and your descendants shall always be welcome in Faerie." She bows to them and turns away.

Perian flashes Ruby a grin and turns to follow his mistress. The faerie host part for their queen and she leads them back into the misty darkness of the gate. As they fade into shadows, a slight figure stops and turns to look back at Ruby. He is slender, shorter than Perian, and dressed in a coat of russet and brown. He has hazel green eyes and in his hand is a carved wooden flute. He puts the flute to his lips and gives a trill of high, chirruping song like a sparrow's call. He raises his hand and slips out of sight.

Davey looks up at the chalk giant carved into the hillside.

"Is this really the Waking World?" he asks.

"We're far from Cornwall," says Ruby. She points away to the East, where the stars are fading." But we are in our world. The sun will be up soon."

"How long was I in Faerie?" he asks. "It seems only yesterday that we rode down into Smith's Den."

"You've been gone half a year," says Ruby.

Davey looks over at Lucy Cotton.

"Thank you both, for bringing me back."

There comes the sound of thudding hooves and they turn to see a pair of horses galloping over the field towards them. One is Dervish, the second is Squire Colby's white stallion.

"They've come to carry us home," says Ruby.

Ruby puts her hand up to Dervish's neck and the chestnut mare nuzzles into her, making a soft huffing noise. The white stallion waits a little way off, watching patiently. When Lucy puts her hand out to him, he comes forward and sniffs at it, unafraid.

"The curse really is gone," she says, grinning.

Davey stands looking at the stars, sharp and clear in the depths of the winter sky. He drinks in the scents of the earth and the nearby wood. He closes his eyes and feels the cold wind on his cheeks.

It is good to be home.

As he turns to go after Ruby and Lucy his foot strikes against something lying on the grass. He bends down and picks up a silver bottle, inlaid with jewels and engraved with an intricate pattern of curling leaves and Faerie script. Davey traces the words and hears their meaning sing in his mind. He uncorks the bottle and sniffs at the faerie wine. It smells of strawberries and summer grass, of apples, grapes and burned sugar. For a moment, Davey is transported back to the Twilight Land. He hears the music of the Fey in the leafy glades of Queen Mab's palace and feels the tug of Faerie magic.

The wine smells sweet but it is not as sweet as the wind on his face and the sight of Ruby as she stands whispering to Dervish. He replaces the stopper and puts the faery wine away into his coat.

Rosie Twigg shrugs off the blanket and creeps out from the cubby hole under the sink where the cook has made up her bed. The kitchen is lit only by the embers of the dying fire and the house is quiet, save for the faint sound of snoring from the servant's room down the passage. Rosie tip-toes over to the pantry and turns the doorknob. She opens the door, reaches up for the back door key and lifts it off its hook.

The cook's name is Nettie and she is a kind woman. She gave Rosie boiled potatoes and bread and jam for dinner.

"I'll tell the Master that she's my niece," Nettie told the housemaid. "We can train her up to be a Kitchen Help."

All of them were kind to Rosie. The gardener found the wooden box to make her a bed and Myrtle, the housemaid, fetched blankets and an old dress that the Master's daughter had outgrown.

"I was going to tear it up for dusters," Myrtle said. "But there's plenty of wear in it."

The dress is pale blue with a silk pocket. Threadbare, with a tear in the hem, it is the nicest thing that Rosie has ever worn. She puts her hand into the pocket and feels the silky lining, cool and smooth against her finger tips.

Rosie hates to trick the kind cook. She wishes that she could stay here forever and be a real Kitchen Help. Jimmy could share the box with her and he could be the gardener's boy. It would be a fine life, with jam and potatoes and a warm place to sleep.

Rosie bites her lip and takes tight hold of the cold iron key. There's no sense in dreaming; if she doesn't do as Famish says then Jimmy will get a beating. She has no choice.

Rosie creeps to the back door and slips the key into the lock. She has to use both hands to turn it and the noise of the catch clicking back makes her jump. She pulls on the handle and the heavy door swings open.

The garden is dark, the moon a faint smudge behind the clouds. Two shadows slip out from the darkness under the trees and Rosie sees Patch and Ned come creeping toward the house.

She hides under the sink while the two men do their work. She pulls the blanket over her head, closes her eyes and stays as still as she can. She wonders if Mr Famish will let her keep the blue dress with the yellow silk pocket?

When Ned nudges her with his foot, Rosie crawls out from under the sink and follows the men outside. She can smell brandy on their breath and knows that they have been helping themselves to more than silver.

At the back wall of the garden, Ned climbs up first and Patch lifts Rosie over. As Ned takes hold of her she turns to take a last look at the house where she dreamt, for a few hours, of being happy. Ned drops her roughly onto the cobbles and she falls into a heap, scraping her knees. She sobs and gives a tiny whimper of pain.

"Shut yer noise," hisses Ned Bones."And get up on your feet. I ain't carryin' you."

  They are almost at the end of the alley when a dark figure steps out in front of them. Ned and Patch stop in their tracks, reaching for their knives. The robber wears a black cloak and hat and his face is covered by a scarf. In his hand is a pistol.
"I'll thank you gentlemen to put down your bags ," says the man. "Drop those shivs too. Nice and slow. Keep your hands where I can see them."
"What's your game?" snarls Ned, sizing up the robber. The masked figure is half his size and his voice is soft; most likely he's just a boy.
Neither man drops their knives. The boy is alone and at such close range its good odds they'll be able to knock him down before he can get a shot off.
"Mr Famish don't take kindly to poachers," says Patch menacingly. "Get back home to your mother before we break your head."
A second cloaked figure steps out beside the first, identically dressed, with a pistol to match. There is a shuffle of boots on the cobbles behind them and Rosie turns to see a third robber with a pistol in his hand. At the robber's side stands a huge, silver-grey wolf.
  Rosie gives a gasp of fright and Patch and Ned exchange stunned looks. The first robber stands aside, gesturing with his pistol.
"Drop the booty. Leave the girl and take to your heels," he says. "You might escape with your lives. Otherwise..."

The silver wolf stalks forward, drawing back its lips and snarling. Patch and Ned drop their sacks with a clatter and run for their lives. The wolf makes a sound half way between a growl and a laugh and bounds after them, passing so close to Rosie that she feels the cool swish of its fur against her face.

The black cloaked figures close in and Rosie whimpers with terror.

"There's no need to fear us," says a gentle voice. Rosie peeps out through her fingers to see the first robber crouching in front of her. The robber pulls down the scarf and takes off the hat and Rosie sees that the robber is a girl. She's about fourteen years old, with long dark hair and kind brown eyes.

"We've come to take you away," says the robber girl. "Jimmy is waiting for you in the carriage, just up the lane."

"Jimmy?"

Rosie stares at the robber girl in wonder. She feels as if she is in a dream.

"Take the sacks to the house," says the brown eyed girl to the other robbers. "Leave them by the back door. With any luck the servants will be able to put the stuff back before anyone notices." She turns to Rosie, smiles and puts out her hand. "Come on."

"Where are you taking me?" asks Rosie.

"Somewhere better than this," says the robber girl.

The carriage stands in a clearing in the wood. The robber girl opens the door and lifts Rosie up inside. On the carriage seat is Jimmy, wide eyed and smiling. Rosie runs to him and buries her face in his chest.

A moment later the two other robbers come running down the lane, followed by a pale girl in a grey cloak.

One of the robbers jumps up onto the carriage's driving seat, while the other climbs inside with the grey cloaked girl. The robber pulls off his scarf and hat and flashes Rosie a grin. He's about the same age as the robber girl and handsome, with brown curly hair and a reckless glint in his blue eyes. The grey cloaked girl is a couple of years younger. Thin and small with a secret fierceness to her that makes Rosie think of a wild beast.

"We'll make a highwayman of you yet, Davey," laughs the robber girl.

"I'd be happy enough with that," says the twinkle eyed boy. "As long as we always steal from scoundrels."

The three of them laugh and the carriage pulls away onto the lane.

The robbers are not what Rosie expected at all; they laugh easily and their faces are kind. She notices that they each wear a medallion about their necks; a circle of gold with an animal inside. The robber girl's charm shows a running horse, the twinkly eyed boy has a hawk and the grey girl has a leaping hare with a moonstone for an eye.

Rosie turns to Jimmy.

"What's happening?" she whispers.

"This is Ruby Gilbert," says Jimmy, pointing to the brown eyed robber girl. "I told you about her. She's an enchantress. They're taking us to her uncle's place."

"But Mr Famish will find us," says Rosie. "He'll know that we betrayed him and -"
"After tonight," says Ruby Gilbert. "You won't need to worry about Mr Famish ever again."

* * * * * *

Charlie Angel pauses at the door, his hand poised to knock, his heart thumping with terror. He's breathing hard from the climb up the narrow stair and his legs are shaking. It's a week since Solomon Phoenix took the bullet from his shoulder and the wound is healing up nicely. His shoulder still aches but the blood stained sling that supports his right arm is just for show.
"I can hear you breathing," comes a harsh voice from beyond the door. "Show yourself, vermin."
Charlie takes a deep breath and pushes open the door.
"You've a nerve coming back here," mutters Mr Famish. He leans forward in his chair, his pointed fingernails digging into the rotting fabric of the arms. "Patch Williams says you ratted us out and scarpered with the Gilbert Boy. He said you tried to kill Ned Bones."
"Patch is a scab arsed Judas," says Charlie. "He was more interested in knocking back rum than stopping Tom Gilbert escape. He's the one who let him out of the cellar and he's the one who shot me in the back when I was up on the wagon doing all I could to stop

the boy escaping. As for Ned," Charlie shrugs, wincing with pain as his shoulder twinges. "Ned Bones knocked himself out on the doorpost. He always had mud for brains."

"You've been gone a week."

"Where've you been hiding?"

"I fell into the back of the wagon after Patch shot me," says Charlie."I don't think Tom Gilbert even knew I was there, bleeding my life out as he rattled back to London. I slipped out at Kennington Turnpike. I was in a bad way and I would have pegged it for sure if this old dear hadn't taken pity on me and taken me in." Charlie sinks to his knees, seemingly weak with pain and exhaustion. "I rested up for a few days but once I had my wits back I remembered what you told me. I went to Josia Colby's place in Chelsea." He takes a sacking bag from his coat. "There wasn't much there."

"What did you get?" asks Mr Famish.

Charlie reaches into the sack and hands Mr Famish a bundle of scorched papers tied up with a leather strap. With them is a silver snuffbox and a small silk bag. Famish leafs through the papers and puts them in his pocket with the snuffbox. He tips the contents of the silk bag onto his palm to show a handful of silver coins.

"Where's the rest?" says Mr Famish. "Josia Colby was as rich as Solomon. Where's the rest of the loot, you thieving runt?"

Famish shoots out his hand, takes hold of Charlie's injured shoulder and gives it twist. Charlie gives a whimper of pain that is only half faked.

"There was nothing else," he gasps. "They must have cleared the place out before they left."

Mr Famish takes Charlie by the throat with one hand and pulls him close, his other hand rummaging through Charlie's jacket. In an inside pocket he finds a silver bottle.

"You twisting little scum," says Famish. "I knew you were holding out on me." He throws Charlie to the floor and lifts the bottle up in the lantern light. The silver patterns shimmer and the gems sparkle.

"This is a pretty thing," says Famish. He shakes the bottle. "What's inside?"

"Dunno," says Charlie. He is kneeling in front of Famish's chair, his eyes on the floor.

Mr Famish kicks him hard in the ribs.

"I asked you, what's inside?"

"Wine," cries Charlie. "I only had a drop, just to try it."

Mr Famish unstops the bottle and sniffs. A faraway look comes into his eyes and he seems to forget Charlie for a moment.

"It don't smell like ordinary plonk," he says, looking thoughtfully down at Charlie. "What was it like?"

"I never tasted wine like it," says Charlie.

"Get up and have another swig," says Famish. "I want to see you drink some down."

Charlie gets slowly to his feet and takes the silver bottle. He knows what the wine is - Davey told him when they hatched the plan - but it is too late to back out. He does not care if he dies; he is willing to risk everything to put an end to Mr Famish and win back Tom and Ruby's trust.

Charlie Angel is a past master at hiding his true intent but keeping his face blank as he raises the faerie wine to his mouth is the greatest con trick that he has ever pulled off. He touches the rim of the bottle to his lips smells the wine for the first time. It smells of fire and spices, of honey and gold. It smells of friendship and of freedom.

Charlie tips the bottle back but before a single drop can reach his lips, Mr Famish grabs the bottle from his hand. Eyes bright with greed, Mr Famish shoves Charlie back against the wall.

"Fetch me a glass from the cabinet," he says. "Make sure it's clean."

Charlie does as he is told and goes to the scruffy cupboard where Famish keeps his special treasures. Among the gold and silver trinkets is a blue Venetian wine glass shaped like a budding crocus. Charlie hands the glass to Mr Famish, dropping his gaze as he does so, not trusting his eyes to hide his true feelings.

"This stuff is too good for a guttersnipe like you," smirks Mr Famish. "But I'll let you watch me drink it."

Mr Famish pours out a generous measure of wine into the glass. He raises it to his nose, closes his eyes and sniffs. He sighs and holds the glass up before the lantern, marvelling at the way the wine catches the light. He puts the glass to his lips and drinks the faerie wine down in a single gulp.

"Very fine," says Mr Famish, wiping his mouth on the sleeve of his jacket.

Silence falls in the mean little room and Mr Famish sits staring into the lantern flame, his eyes looking out into a place the Charlie can only guess at. The sharp lines of the old man's face seem to soften and a hint of a smile plays about his lips. Charlie is not sure that he believes it; but he sees a tear form in the corner of Mr Famish's eye and roll slowly down his parched cheek.

Hooves clatter on the cobbles below and a carriage rattles over the bridge. A man shouts, a woman laughs, and still Mr Famish sits in silence.

And then, without a word, Mr Famish stands and walks to the door. He does not look at Charlie. He seems not to know that he is there. He opens the door and walks away down the winding stair. As Mr Famish's footfalls fade, Charlie steps to the window and pulls back the curtain. A moment later he sees Mr Famish step out into the street and walk away over London Bridge.

Mr Famish has no thought for where he is heading, he simply lets his feet lead him. The Faerie wine is in his blood and he is remembering things long forgotten. The wine brings Mr Famish the taste of birdsong and of starlight, it brings him memories of joyful laughter and of bare feet running on new spring grass. It brings back the sweetness of his mother's smile, lost to him all these years. The twisted greed that has driven him for so long is gone, and he is a child again.

Mr Famish walks on, down through Lambeth and Kennington. He does not feel the cold of the night and he does not see the houses or the people that he passes in the darkness. The passersby, in turn, do not notice him, their eyes sliding away as if he were already gone from the world.

Long ago the whole of the land of Albion was covered in a great wild wood, running from one rocky shore to another. In that wooded land there were many paths. Some led from the Waking World into Faerie, others ran into places for which we have forgotten the names. Most of the Faerie paths were lost, long ago, buried under fields and fences, beneath the sprawl of the city and the tangle of roads. The gates between the worlds are all but gone, but a few remain, if you know where to look, in the forgotten places that have slipped off the corners of the maps.

Mr Famish passes on, towards his heart's desire, out through Brixton, past the sleeping villages and farms. As the frost falls on the grass and the eastern sky begins to brighten, he stumbles into a forgotten glade deep in a tangly wood. In the heart of the glade stands a tall grey stone. The carvings on the stone have faded with the passing centuries but the swirling shapes are still there, like fingerprints under the moss. Mr Famish walks through the ankle deep drifts of dusty leaves. He passes under the shadow of the stone and is gone from the Waking World.

If you have enjoyed this book then please consider leaving a review wherever you bought it. Good reviews help to sell books and the more books that I sell, the more time I will have to spend writing new ones.

You can sign up to my mailing list to hear about the latest publications. You will also get a key to the Secret Glade, where you will find exclusive stories and other great stuff to download for free.
Go to **www.deepdarkforest.net** and click on the links.

You can follow me on:
Twitter @AJMwriter
Facebook@dreamsfromtheforest

I am always happy to get feedback from readers.

You can email me at -
deepdarkforest@icloud.com

www.ingramcontent.com/pod-product-compliance
Lightning Source LLC
Chambersburg PA
CBHW032120170626
46808CB00006B/2030